Praise for Bianca D'Arc's *Lords of the Were*

"...a thrill ride from start to finish...The love scenes are scorching and filled with tenderness that helps make these characters so enchanting. Action packed and simply delightful, Ms. D'Arc has created another wonderful world that readers will be anxious to visit again."

~ Water Nymph, Literary Nymphs Reviews

4 Stars! "With an interesting premise and intriguing characters, *Lords of the Were* has all the makings of a wonderful paranormal erotic romance...This beautifully executed novel offers plenty of steamy potential for the installments to come."

~ Claire Skye, Just Erotic Romance Reviews

"Until now, I would have told you that the Dragon Knights series was my favorite from Bianca D'Arc, but with the release of *Lords of the Were*, she launches a new series called *Tales of the Were* which has quickly tied for first place in my favors with the Dragon Knights series!...succeeds in turning the ménage concept into a beautiful love story with plenty of steam!"

~ Jennifer, CK2S Kwips and Kritiques

Lords of the Were

Bianca D'Arc

A Samhain Publishing, Ltd. publication.

Samhain Publishing, Ltd.
2932 Ross Clark Circle, #384
Dothan, AL 36301
www.samhainpublishing.com

Lords of the Were
Copyright © 2006 by Bianca D'Arc
Print ISBN: 1-59998-351-6
Digital ISBN: 1-59998-160-2

Editing by Jessica Bimberg
Cover by Anne Cain

First Samhain Publishing, Ltd. electronic publication: October 2006
First Samhain Publishing, Ltd. print publication: January 2007

Dedication

To my family for sticking by me as I chase my dream.

Also to the many new friends I've made along this journey. Much love to Jess, Sharon, Jeanette, Jennifer, Suzette, Serena, Megan, Rene, Stacy, and a multitude of others. You guys are the best!

Chapter One

Allie puffed as she tromped through the dark woods at Betina's side. It was All Hallows Eve, the night little American kids ran around in funny outfits gorging on candy, but to her mother's people, it was a serious time. The turning of the year, the night when spirits roamed more freely than at any other point on the wheel of the year. The old ones called it Samhain, though many misconceptions about the old ways and beliefs had arisen over the years.

"Are you sure we're safe up here?" Allie looked nervously around the dark woods. Born in the city, she'd only recently learned of her legacy. The woods, which had been so pretty and colorful to her earlier in the day, suddenly seemed ominous and threatening.

Betina finally stopped, just shy of a large clearing. Before them stretched a nearly perfect ring of ancient stones overgrown with vines and plants, but still vaguely recognizable. A large flat-topped slab of rock stood in the center, seeming somehow otherworldly. A wispy shroud of fog rose around it, lighting the mossy surface with an ethereal glow.

"We are servants of the Lady. We'll be safe here, honoring Her. It's time you took your rightful place, Allesandra. It's nearly too late already."

The older woman's cryptic words sent a small shiver down Allie's spine. She wasn't used to speaking so openly about her somewhat unconventional beliefs. She had a decent career as an accountant, making a good living serving private clients out of her home office. All she really needed to do her work was her laptop and a phone, so her business was portable enough to allow her this time away from the city to learn more about her mother's life and the friends she'd left behind.

Having learned only recently that her mother had been a priestess in some kind of secret society had been shocking enough. But then to learn Allie was expected to take her place as a priestess sometime during her thirty-second year had been downright scary, to say the least. Still, something in Allie responded to the idea, urging her to follow where her mother's last requests led, no matter how bizarre they sounded to the city-girl accountant who tried to present a rather dull facade to the rest of the world. Underneath the surface lurked a woman who believed in the old ways and hid a wild nature, never letting loose, always keeping a low profile.

When Betina, her mother's old friend, finally tracked Allie down and told her about her "sacred duty", at first Allie had been skeptical. Then Betina had given her a slender book. It turned out to be a journal in her mother's hand, written before she'd died so young. Allie knew her mother's handwriting from the similar small book she'd had since she was a teen. It had been held in trust and secrecy by her mother's attorney until Allie turned thirteen.

In it, her mother had described the old religion that had come to mean so much to Allie as she'd entered young adulthood. Never acknowledging her mother's non-standard beliefs in the open, Allie had nonetheless found a way to resolve her own belief in the goddess her mother wrote about with the religion she'd been exposed to by her adoptive parents.

The tenets weren't so horribly different. Peace and goodwill were sought along with protection from evil. Allie didn't see anything contradictory with what her mother had believed. Her mother had gone out of her way to teach her child the origins and similarities between the old ways and the current popular religions. Allie had often wondered if her mother hadn't somehow known she would die young and not have a chance to teach her child these things herself.

The book was a cherished link to her mother, filled with insight documenting her mother's own journey to some kind of spiritual peace. But on certain points it was rather vague. Those points were clarified by the new volume Betina gave her to study. Betina had delivered the book, then left Allie alone for a few days to read it and think it all through. The time was much needed.

By the time Betina returned, Allie knew she had to follow the unexpected path laid before her. She had to see where her mother's hopes for her would lead. Allie agreed to go with Betina, packed up her laptop and notified her clients, then took off for what promised to be a great adventure.

Which led her to this creepy, overgrown circle of stones on All Hallows Eve.

Allie's mother had left words of wisdom and a rough account of her life and beliefs. Beliefs, Allie realized only now, which explained many of the odd things in her own life and the strange power she sometimes felt within her, trying to get out.

In the months since they'd met, Betina had shown Allie how to tap into that power, and Allie believed more strongly than ever in the power of the old ways. She was coming to understand things about the world she'd always taken for granted, and things about herself she'd always felt, but never fully comprehended. Allie knew in her heart respecting her mother's wishes was the right thing, and that was just one of the many reasons she'd trudged up this cold mountain with Betina on a spooky Halloween night.

It was also her birthday. Just at midnight, Allie would turn thirty-three, so in order fulfill her mother's wishes, they had to do the ceremony tonight. Betina, as high priestess, would run the show. She had somehow convinced Allie to do this the old way, in the presence of the wild creatures of the forest, though Allie would have preferred to be indoors, out of the chill night air.

Betina caught Allie's hand and her wandering attention, stepping them into the circle of stones purposefully, side by side. It was only then Allie realized there were animals all around the clearing, looking in, or perhaps standing sentinel. She wasn't sure where the idea came from, but she saw the sparkling eyes of what she thought must be wolves and other creatures flickering in the darkness.

"We're not alone out here, Betty."

Allie's nerves were stretched taut. She wasn't much used to animals, having lived in an apartment most of her life, and the idea of wild animals that could pounce on her at any time freaked her out a little.

Betina laughed and the sound rang through the small clearing like the tinkling of bells. For an older woman, Betina had a very fey look about her. She was quite a bit shorter than Allie's five foot five, with tousled curls that were only just starting to show streaks of white, and a face that simply beamed. She was ethereally pretty and just standing next to her made Allie feel like a big, giant lump. Allie always felt rather average, but Betina's otherworldly beauty only emphasized the vast differences between the two women.

Allie's baby fine hair was a dark golden color, and her eyes were as blue as the sky, large and deep set. Her figure was on the voluptuous side with wide hips, large breasts and a curvy waist, and she fell far short of the reed-thin model standard everyone seemed to think was perfection.

"We are never alone, Allesandra. Fear not Her creatures. The *were* come to witness, guard and protect. They serve the Lady as we do."

Allie didn't always understand everything Betina talked about, but she'd learned through their meditation practice to trust the older woman. Betina knew things that could not be explained by science, things Allie had only just begun to experience and do herself.

As she spoke, Betina unbuttoned the robe she'd worn on the trek through the woods. She'd told Allie they'd have to do this ceremony in the nude—or "skyclad" as she called it. Allie hadn't been thrilled with the idea, but seeing as it was only the two of them and a few animals as witnesses, she wasn't going to argue. Allie followed Betina's lead and was soon standing naked under the stars, near the stone altar, next to the smaller woman.

For a woman who had to be at least her mother's age, Betina was still amazingly beautiful, with a great body. Allie was glad no one else could see them. Well, no one except the animals all around—but they were just animals. Surely they wouldn't gossip about her big hips.

Betina had prepared her in advance for the ceremony and the steps they would perform both separately and together. Allie knew her role and set about consecrating the circle as Betina had taught her. Immediately after she closed the circle, she felt the cold bite of the autumn air lessen and a now-familiar stillness enter her being which would aid her in the next steps she must take.

The power bubbled up from inside, stronger than ever before. An awareness of the magic outside the circle came to her through newly expanded senses. It was the magic of the forest creatures, she realized, sparing a moment to look around the circle and see with new eyes the soft glow of their auras. Golden rainbows of light shimmered here and there as she registered the odd collection of creatures observing the two naked women inside the sacred circle.

There were wolves and big mountain cats, coyotes, bears and even a few huge raptors in the trees, among others. Truly an odd assortment to be socializing so close together in harmony, yet they looked comfortable in each other's presence, watching the women in the circle.

Betina started to chant, calling Allie back to task as she took her place near the altar and sang with the older woman. Betina's voice tinkled merrily through the clearing, and Allie's flowed. It was her one pride, her voice. Allie sang every chance she got and had even done some professional chorus work with one of the larger opera companies when she'd lived in New York City. Her voice surged and blended, chiming clear through the circle, building the power of which she was only just becoming fully aware.

She'd never felt so much power before. The very earth pulsed in the stone of the altar, in the loamy grass beneath her feet and in the heartbeats of the animals who stood as the only witnesses all around.

"It is time." Betina's voice startled her as the song faded into silence. "We are nearly at the turning of the year and the moment of your birth, Allesandra. We must act quickly now."

Allie knew what she had to do. Taking a deep breath for courage, she stepped up to the surprisingly clean slab of stone and lay down on the natural altar. Betina moved away, out of her sight for a short moment. When she returned, she began a new song in an ancient tongue, opening her satchel and scattering herbs into the air in four directions. She anointed Allie's forehead with a special oil mixture they'd prepared together, just days before.

Allie felt as if she were sinking into the stone as Betina's song ended and she spoke words about the ancient forest and the Lady they served. Allie felt the power of the earth flowing up through the stone and into her being. It was a sensation she'd never even imagined, but it felt somehow familiar and welcoming.

"I stand for the fey and the human, and for the Lady," Betina intoned, rubbing a star symbol with the oil onto Allie's head. "I beseech the Lady to take this mind and fill it. Welcome Her servant and imbue her with knowledge and wisdom."

Betina fell back and suddenly there were two other presences beside Allie, one on either side. She tried to jerk in surprise, but it was like she was glued to the stone slab. She couldn't speak either. She was in fact, completely paralyzed and helpless. Allie didn't like the feeling at all and feared what might come next. Her wide eyes searched out the newcomers and found two striking men, identical in looks and as naked as she, standing on either side of her. Betina handed one the pot of oil.

"We stand for the *were* of sky and land. We serve the Lady and protect Her priestesses." The man's deep voice washed over her senses as he dipped his large fingers into the oil and passed the pot over her body to his companion, his twin. "We beseech the Lady to take this heart," his fingers moved over her breast, the warm oil dripping as he traced the sacred symbol over her heart, "and fill it. Welcome Her servant and imbue her with compassion and love."

"We beseech the Lady to take this vessel," the other man spoke, his voice equally firm and oddly alluring as he trailed his warm, oiled fingers just below her belly button, "and fill it. Welcome Her servant and imbue her with fertility and strength."

Allie wanted to object, but when the man's strong hand rubbed that slick sign over her belly, her insides turned to molten lava. Her very womb quivered and a sultry dampness seeped from deep within. The aroma of her desire was pungent in the air and both men inhaled strongly, pleased expressions entering their eyes as they looked down at her, long and hard.

That wasn't the only thing that was long and hard, either. She could see them both clearly as they stepped back from the altar. Both men were built on the large side of gorgeous with long, thick cocks that under other circumstances probably would have made her gasp with appreciation. As it stood, her vocal chords seemed to be frozen, and she was still completely immobilized on the altar. The only things she could move were her eyes.

Betina came back into her line of vision and took up a new chant. The men joined her after the first section and the deep timbres of their voices sent warm shivers of appreciation down her spine. Both men watched her, eying her body and meeting her gaze with not one shred of timidity. These were alpha males, she realized, strong in their own masculinity and truly appreciative of all that was feminine.

Betina spoke more but Allie heard very little, consumed as she was by the men who watched her so closely. At one point Betina placed her hand over Allie's eyes, forcing them closed and a lightness entered her body, seeping up from the stone of the altar, making her feel freer and more powerful than she ever had before. As the sensation faded, Betina removed her hand and Allie suddenly realized she could move again. She turned her head first, taking stock of the clearing.

The men were gone, but two huge wolves stood waiting, one on either side of the altar where she had last seen the men.

"Rise, Allesandra, newest priestess of the Lady."

Betina's words prompted her to sit up. Allie had to steady herself by grabbing the edges of the stone as she swung her legs down to one side. She was a little dizzy, but otherwise felt great. To be certain, she felt different than she had before the ceremony, but she didn't quite understand what had changed. Betina would explain it all to her, she knew, given time.

Betina walked to the head of the stone slab and motioned for Allie to stand at the foot. After one false start due to her still spinning senses, Allie took her position, noting the wolves stayed one on either side, watching all. They were massive beasts, larger than she thought any wild wolf would be, though she'd never seen one in the flesh before.

As her stance steadied, the wolves watched, their eyes never leaving her. It made her nervous, but she still had a bit of the residual power from the altar running through her system so nothing bothered her too much. Her thinking was somehow accelerated and softened at the same time. One part of her mind realized she should be far more nervous about the wild creatures watching her so hungrily, but the part of her mind that seemed to be in charge at the moment thought nothing of it. It was like some new entity that was far wiser than Allie had taken up residence in her mind and was influencing her thoughts.

"Sister Allesandra, would you perform the blessing?" Betina requested.

Allie knew the words and motions to the ritual blessing. It had been one of the first things Betina taught her, but the form of address was new. Betina had never called her "sister" before, though she'd referred to Allie's mother and a few other priestesses that way.

Allie nodded and raised her arms skyward, palms up and open as she breathed deeply, seeking her center and focusing her energy. It was easier than it had ever been before and she actually felt the energy flowing through her. For the first time she felt she was truly a vessel—a tool of the Lady—the way Betina had told her it would be. Closing her eyes, Allie briefly savored the sensation, entertaining rainbows of light behind her eyelids. When her eyes opened, the rainbows were still there, only they were shooting strongly from her raised arms through the circle and out into the trees beyond, touching the woodland creatures that had gathered to bear witness to her ceremony.

At once a great howl went up from the wolves still in the clearing, to be echoed by their friends deeper in the woods. Coyotes yowled, bears growled and big cats roared and screeched. Owls hooted and raptors cried, raising their voices with their brethren in a cacophony of sound that lasted only a few minutes while the rainbows of light from her hands touched them all.

Allie's eyes widened in wonder as she completed the motions of the blessing, watching the rainbow sparks dissipate and scatter. The older woman was grinning from ear to ear, her hands clasped together in front of her heart in an expression of joy.

"Let the *were* bear witness to this young priestess' gift and spread the word to all your brethren. Lilias is reborn in her daughter. She must be protected."

Oddly then, the wolves bowed to Betina, stretching forward on their front legs and lowering their sleek heads, though their gazes remained fixed on the older woman. Betina bowed her head to them as well, then they rose and moved toward Allie. She took a quick step back in alarm as the huge creatures closed in on her, but something inside said to stand her ground. Both wolves stopped—one on each side of her nude body. The beasts were so large they came up past her waist, and she thought once again these wolves were much larger than she thought they'd be.

They reached forward with their muzzles at the same time, licking her hands and moving forward to brush her bare thighs, waist, and arms with their soft fur, licking and stroking her with their rough tongues. She giggled when they both hit ticklish spots on her abdomen and suddenly she felt the joy in their wildness and saw the humor in their dark, dancing eyes. She stroked them with her hands and even bent forward to kiss one on the nose. She yelped as the other wolf chose that moment to lick his wet tongue over one of her nipples and just that quickly, she found herself remembering those twin men whose touches had so aroused her while she'd been stuck to that altar. Could they have been only a dream?

The wolves caressed her just once more, then both bounded off into the woods, yipping to their companions to follow suit. One by one the watching wild animals left the perimeter of the trees, though not all of them left. Some stayed behind to watch and guard. Or at least, that's the impression she got, though why she should think that, she had no real idea.

Betina walked up to her and handed Allie the robe she'd discarded earlier. Donning it quickly, she saw the older woman was already dressed. The robes were simple, but of fine material that shimmered softly in the full moon's light. Betina had said being consecrated on a full moon was essential and the fact that this year the full moon fell on Halloween, which also happened to be the day of Allie's birth, was a very good omen. Allie turned back to her new mentor.

"Did I do everything right?" Allie asked, somewhat nervous of her performance. Strange things had happened and though at the time everything seemed somewhat hazy, she was slowly beginning to feel more like her normal self and questioning the incredible events of the past hour.

Betina smiled gently as she took Allie by the arm and started back through the trees once more, away from the circle. Allie noticed they weren't going back the way they'd come and raised her eyebrow toward the older woman.

"You were terrific, kid. Perfect, in fact. And yes, we're stopping off somewhere else before we head back to the car. We've been invited to a celebration of sorts and you're the guest of honor."

"Another surprise?" Allie asked with a bit of teasing admonition.

Betina shrugged and linked her arm through Allie's. "You know I would never allow you to come to any harm. I didn't tell you about the twins' part in the ceremony because frankly I wasn't sure they'd come. It's a compliment to you that they did."

Allie stopped short and faced the other woman. "You mean they were real? I almost thought I was hallucinating or something."

Betina's laughter sounded through the misty woods. "Yes, they are quite dreamy, aren't they? But I assure you they're real and they were there, and their presence helped establish your rightful place."

"My rightful place in what?"

"In the world, my little chick. You are on the verge of learning there is much more to the heavens and earth than you have so far believed." They started walking again and Betina took Allie's arm once more. "We'll continue your training, but now you'll also have other teachers. Ones you never would have expected."

"Those two men?"

Betina's smile was almost sinful. "Oh, yes. Among others. But by appearing tonight, they've agreed to my requests. They'll help in your education so you can eventually take your mother's place."

"What did my mother do? I mean, what's expected of me?"

"All in good time." Betina patted her hand. "But just know that it's nothing more than you can handle, and you'll have guides and protectors all along your path. There is some danger to you, now that you're embracing your power, but the danger was always there, just under the surface. The only thing that's kept you safe thus far is the fact that you lived in the city and were well hidden. The minute you moved out here, both sides in our struggle became aware of your presence. Our side, the side of light, wants only to protect you, while the others...well, let's just say they don't have your best interests at heart." Allie was growing alarmed. "But not to worry, even now our protectors move with us through these woods and like me, now you will never walk alone."

"You have guards with you at all times?"

Betina laughed. "Something like that, but it's not the intrusive imposition you're imagining. I am merely cared for and looked after by good folk who would help should evil come upon me. I'm perfectly able to defend myself, but it never hurts to have a helping hand and an extra pair of eyes keeping watch over an old lady."

"You're not old," Allie laughed though the subject was making her wary.

"Little chick, I'll tell you a secret. I was already old when your mother was my student. Such is the power of the Lady we serve. Had she lived, your mother would look much as you do now. Once consecrated, we do not age as others. The Lady preserves our lives as long as She needs us here to do Her work. Judging by the omens of both your birth and now your consecration, I'd say you'll have many years ahead to do Her work."

They walked in silence for a bit, though Allie's mind spun with questions and the things she'd experienced so far that dark Halloween night. After a while she became aware of the soft padding of paws on either side as they made their way through the trees. Once she caught sight of what she thought were the glowing eyes of a big mountain cat, but she couldn't be sure. One thing was certain though, there were big animals walking alongside them, but their presence didn't feel threatening. No, they felt protective more than anything, and for a city girl that was a big leap. She wasn't used to animals of any size dogging her steps and the fact that she was feeling cosseted by the big predators' presence in these dark woods was somewhat alarming.

Allie knew she was much more comfortable with the events of the night than she should be. In another part of her mind though, she felt the rightness of what had happened. It was as if part of her that had been dormant was now awakening and it knew these events were right and good. It was just a gut feeling, but it reassured her.

Before too long, soft yellow light peeped through the dense trees as they approached a small house that backed up right into the forest. Light, laughter and music flowed from the house and the voices of many people spilled forth into the night in welcoming harmony.

"Is that a Halloween party?"

Betina's mischievous smile extended to her eyes. "Of sorts. It's a bit of a housewarming party too, to welcome you to the neighborhood."

"But I live down the mountain, in town." Allie was confused.

Betina wrinkled her nose. "Yes, in that stuffy little apartment. I know. But if you like this house, it's yours. Rent free."

"What?" Allie stopped short as they stepped from the last of the trees into the cozy backyard of the inviting little house. "Why?"

Betina pulled her forward. "The twins own this land and the house. By showing up tonight I knew they were agreeing to let you live here. It's part of what I discussed with them a while back." Betina let go of Allie's arm and held her hands out to enjoy the night breeze. "This is a beautiful spot to live and you'll be safe here, Allie, while you learn how to use your gifts. Plus, it's quiet, so you'll be able to work without disturbance."

Allie often complained about the noise from her neighbors in the small house she shared. She was a city girl, true, but somehow these people were even noisier than all of Manhattan Island when she wanted to get some work done.

A change of scene would be nice. She looked at the light spilling invitingly from the snug dwelling. But could she really take advantage of such kindness from total strangers? Allie was an independent woman and a planner. She'd saved up long and hard to finance her escape from the city. She had money to pay her way and pride demanded she do so.

"I'd like to get out of that apartment, but I won't mooch off people I don't know."

"How about people you do know then?"

The masculine voice from behind had Allie whirling to face the woods. From out of the low hanging branches stepped one of the men who'd taken part in her ceremony, mercifully dressed this time—though the top button on his jeans was undone and his shirt hung open in a way that made heat rise right up from her toes to the top of her head. The man was hot!

Betina laughed at Allie's reaction, stepping forward to hug the man, dwarfed by his huge size.

"Thank you, Rafe. I was worried there for a minute that you and that twin of yours were going to be stubborn."

The man she called Rafe set the smaller woman away from him with a fond smile. "Now you know we had to go through the motions on our end, m'lady. We had to do this the right way. And I'm Tim."

Betina gasped. "Oh, I'm sorry, Timothy. I thought I'd finally gotten over not being able to tell you two apart. Forgive me."

"Nothing to forgive when even our own packmates can't figure out who's who half the time." His smile was tight as he turned to face Allie. "Now, will you accept our hospitality? This house has been standing empty for a few months and no one else in the pack has need at the moment, so it's yours if you want it."

Allie ignored his strange phrasing for the moment and faced the issue, as she saw it, head on. She would not be a freeloader.

"It's really beautiful and I'd like to try living here, but I insist on paying rent."

Tim looked her over and she felt the heat of his gaze, just as if he touched her bare skin with those big hands once again. Her temperature rose and a slickness found its way between her bare thighs under the concealing robe. Tim lifted his head and sniffed as if he could scent her on the crisp evening breeze.

"I'll talk it over with my brother, but we'd like to have you here. It'll save us having to travel into town to assist with your lessons and you'll be safe up here on pack lands."

"Pack?" she repeated, turning to Betina.

"She doesn't have a clue, does she?" Tim asked Betina. Allie felt the heat of anger rise in her body thinking he was disparaging her.

"No, but she learns fast. She has good instincts."

Tim looked her up and down once more before starting for the back porch and the party already in progress. "Let's hope so. For all our sakes."

Chapter Two

Allie steamed as she watched the big man's retreating back. He buttoned his shirt as he went, tucking it in to his unbuttoned jeans before entering the back door of the house. A cheer went up as he entered as if all the people within were greeting him at once and then the buzz of voices returned to its previous raucous level. Allie watched until he was out of sight, powerless to pry her gaze from his commanding figure though she noted he didn't look back even once.

"Let's sit here in the garden for a moment before we go in. I have a few things you should know before we join the others." Betina led her to a small bench hidden among a row of hedges bordering one side of the yard. A bird bath reflected the full moon in front of the bench. A small rose garden off to the side showed its autumn thorns in the bright light of the October moon. Allie sat, trying to get her mind off the disturbing man but Betina's next words brought her thoughts back around to him and his equally disturbing brother.

"Identical twins are not common among the *were*. Twin alphas are even rarer. Rare and magical. Wolf, bear, cougar, jaguar, eagle, hawk, condor, and more all have their twin pairs, but the Lady decides which of the *were*tribes will receive the next alpha twin pair each generation. While those twins are in their prime, they rule over all the *were*tribes in this part of the world, no matter what their form. Often they take mates from among their own tribe, but every once in a while, the pair will mate with a single priestess. Timothy and his brother Rafael are the current prime alpha pair and they are wolves."

"Excuse me?" Was she implying that the people were animals and vice versa?

"The animals you sensed around the circle tonight were *were*. As are Tim and Rafe. The *were*tribes take many forms and almost all serve the Lady. As do we. Long ago, an alliance was formed and the *were*tribes help protect Her servants. Namely us."

"You mean the animals turn into people?"

"More like the people turn into animals." For the second time that night, a deep, masculine voice out of the darkness had Allie turning in surprise. This time it was the other twin brother interrupting their conversation, though he'd taken time to dress fully, tucking his shirt in and buttoning his jeans.

"Tim, go back to the party. You've interrupted us enough for one night." Betina waved her hand at the handsome man and Allie was surprised Betina couldn't tell this man was clearly not the same one they'd spoken with just a few minutes before.

He winked at her and shook his head. "I'm Rafe, m'lady."

Again Betina was embarrassed. "I'm sorry, Rafael. I've done it again."

"No harm done. But your little protégé here seems to need some convincing about the *were*. I'd be happy to help." His roguish grin brought an answering smile to Allie's face before she even realized it. Where his brother annoyed and embarrassed her, this twin appealed to her mischievous side.

"Some would say you've done quite enough for one evening, my friend, but perhaps you're right. Would it tax you to show her the change? She needs to see it, I think."

25

Rafe grinned sexily and began to unbutton his shirt. "Not at all. I'd be happy to oblige."

When he shucked his jeans, he had a raging hard-on that he seemed not in the least inclined to hide. Instead, he moved toward Allie and winked again, his dick bobbing outrageously before he fell to the ground.

At first Allie was alarmed, but became completely astounded and nearly overwhelmed as she watched the man morph into a huge wolf. The same wolf that had licked her nipple earlier that evening, if she were any judge.

"*Were*," she whispered, understanding beginning to dawn. "You mean he's a *were*wolf!" Her voice rose as did her shock. The huge wolf padded up to her and laid his head in her lap, sniffing at the fold of her thighs as if he could smell her previous arousal and was enjoying it. Hell, he probably was. The pervert.

"Yes, that's what I've been trying to tell you. *Were*wolves, *were*cats, *were*bears and more inhabit this forest. They own the land bordering the national park and Rafe here is one of the current prime alpha twin pair. Be flattered he allowed you to witness his change. It's not something they share outside their families very often." Betina reached over to scratch behind Rafe's ear and smiled at him. "Thank you, Rafael. I think that's convinced her."

Rafael moved his head out of her lap and rose to place both front paws on the stone bench, one on either side of Allie's seated body. He swiped his wet tongue over her cheeks as she reached up reflexively and tangled her fingers in his pelt, trying to push him away, laughing at his antics. He was like a huge puppy, buoyant and full of life.

Rafe jumped down and changed back into a man as she watched, licking her lips with appreciation as his naked form took shape before her.

"So, what do you think?" he asked, bending for his jeans as he began dressing.

"It's hard to believe." Allie's voice was tempered with awe. "If I hadn't just seen you change before my eyes..."

Rafe chuckled. "Wait'll you see Rocky."

"Rocky? What's he a *were*raccoon?" Allie's sense of the ridiculous got the better of her as the sarcasm slipped out, but Rafe laughed outright for a good long time. She counted herself lucky he hadn't taken offense at her unguarded words.

"Oh, man! He's going to howl when we tell him that one." Rafe wiped his face and offered her a hand. She took it and stood, Betina watching them carefully. "Rocky's a *were*bear. A grizzly. On second thought, maybe we shouldn't tell him you thought he was a raccoon. Might be safer." Rafe's roguish wink and grin set her completely at ease.

No doubt about it, Rafe was a charmer. He extended a hand to help Betina stand too, and Allie noted he was polite as well. He was so much different from his brother, yet they were identical in looks down to the last detail.

"Has Jilly arrived yet, do you know?" Betina asked him as she rose.

"No, but Thomas is chafing to meet his kin."

"Allie," Betina faced her and the older woman's eyes were shadowed for the first time that night, "I want you to understand that I promised your mother to keep you away from everything connected with your heritage until you were of age. That meant keeping you from your family as well. When your mother died and her mates with her, they left behind some family that would have claimed you, but your mother felt you'd be in too much danger. She made me promise to take you away from here and put you in a foster home."

"I knew the Petersons weren't my real parents, but they were good to me. I can't believe they hid the existence of blood relations from me for all these years, though."

Allie felt betrayed by the family that had raised her and Rafe placed a warm arm around her shoulder that was surprisingly comforting. She didn't question his right to touch her so familiarly. Instead she snuggled into his warmth, needing his strength after this latest revelation. It had been a night of discovery, learning that things she'd always believed to be true were not.

Betina sighed. "They didn't know. Don't be mad at them. If anyone should feel your anger and hurt, it's me, but I made a promise to your mother and I followed her wishes."

Something Betina had said finally registered as odd in Allie's mind and she raised confused eyes to her mentor. "You said my mother's mates—plural—what in the world are you talking about? I was told my father died at the same time as my mother."

"That's true. But your mother had two mates." Betina looked up at Rafe as if asking for help in explaining and Allie raised her eyes to his as he squeezed her shoulders.

"Your mother was mated to the ruling alpha twin pair before Tim and me. They were *were*cats named Jason and William. They were your sires and they died protecting you and your mother. When they died, Tim and I had to take control of the tribes before our time, but we managed to keep our people together. Your mother and her mates have been sorely missed."

Allie could hardly believe what they were saying. She had two fathers? It didn't seem real, yet she'd met Tim and Rafe and they certainly were real enough. Could her mother have married two men? It was totally unconventional, but then her mother's entire life was unconventional. Her belief system, her activities, her career—if you could call being a priestess a career in the traditional sense—her friends, and all the rest. Somehow it didn't seem too farfetched to believe her mother might've had two men like Tim and Rafe as her life companions.

"And they had brothers and sisters? I have aunts and uncles I've never met?"

Betina nodded. "One aunt and one uncle still living. Another of your uncles died in the same attack, trying to defend your mother and fathers. His name was Peter and he was a bit older than your sires. Thomas was their younger brother and Jilly their younger sister. They both have cubs now with their mates, so you have a number of cousins too."

"Who can change into big cats?" Allie shook her head in wonder. She could hardly believe everything she'd seen and done this night, but somewhere inside her the pieces were falling into place, making her feel things were finally going right in her world.

"Cougars," Rafe clarified, stroking his arm away from her shoulders as he took her hand and started walking toward the house. "And they're anxious to meet you."

But Allie stopped short, causing Betina and Rafe to stop also and look at her flushed face.

"You mean to tell me all those people saw me naked?" Rafe laughed and even Betina laughed, but Allie was outraged. "Dammit, Betty! You told me we'd be all alone up there."

Betina grinned and tried to calm her protégé. "I didn't know they'd all come to the ceremony. I wasn't even sure Rafe and his twin would show up until the last minute."

"But you knew it was a possibility!"

Betina held up her hands, palms outward. "You're right and I'm sorry. I've sprung a lot on you tonight, but I honestly didn't see any other way of breaking this all to you. Before the consecration, I don't think you would have believed any of it, but now with the Lady's power awakening within you, you're more able to take it in and feel what is true and what is not." Betina took Allie's free hand in hers. "I will never mislead you again, Allesandra. This I promise you."

Allie felt somewhat mollified by Betina's promise but still appalled to think all those people had seen her in her birthday suit. On her birthday. How appropriate. Allie's face flamed even as Rafael cupped her hot cheek in his palm.

"Don't fret, Allie. Nudity is just not a big deal among the *were*. We have to be nude when we shift and we shift all the time. It's part of who we are. If you hang around us long enough, you'll get used to our ways." His smile turned devilish. "Besides, you've got nothing to be worried about. You're gorgeous, little priestess, and believe me, every male *were* at your ceremony enjoyed seeing your pretty young tits."

Betina smacked his arm and he stepped back playfully. "That's enough out of you, Rafe. The girl's already embarrassed enough. Don't tease her." Betina turned back to Allie. "Now, are you ready to meet your family?"

Allie shrugged, though she couldn't forget that this man, in wolf form, had licked her nipple earlier that night. A shiver raced down her spine that had little to do with fear and much to do with excitement. But she had other things to attend to first. She was eager to meet her long-lost family and at the same time, definitely *not* looking forward to facing a house full of people who'd seen her naked only an hour before.

"Ready as I'll ever be, I guess."

The same cheer of greeting engulfed them as she and Betty entered the house with Rafael a few minutes later. Betina introduced her to people as they passed in a whirlwind of names and faces, but Betina had a goal and they were making their way towards it. Allie became aware of Tim taking up a position on her other side as Rafe stayed to their right, flanking them as if protecting the two small women making their way through the crowd. Oddly, she felt reassured by the twins' presence though she'd only just met them both.

At long last, Betina ushered her into the front room of the house and walked right up to a tall, lanky man who stood in profile. Allie knew instantly this man was her uncle. He had Allie's same tawny coloring and wavy golden hair. His profile was an older, more masculine version of her own, but when he turned to face her, the delight in his deep golden eyes made her breath catch in her throat. She had blue eyes and softer features, but other than that, she was looking in a slightly distorted, masculine mirror.

The man drew near with a single bounding step, uncommonly light on his feet. He reached out with one large hand to cup her shoulder.

"You're the image of your fathers," his voice cracked with emotion as he pulled her into his strong arms and hugged her close, "but you have your mother's eyes. Sweet Allesandra, how we've missed you."

Allie felt her heart hinge open and tears rolled down her face as she clung to the older man. He was strong and his arms felt safe and warm, like she imagined her father would have felt had he—no, make that *they*—lived to raise her.

"You're my Uncle Thomas," Allie whispered softly as she returned his welcoming hug.

He let her go and held her at arm's length for a long moment, looking deeply into her eyes. Then he turned her around so she stood in front of him facing the room full of watching *were*.

"This woman is blood of my blood. I stand in place of her sires and claim her as my own. I will protect her where my brothers cannot."

A roar of approval met his words and though Allie was still a bit confused, she realized he'd just claimed her publicly. He turned her back around, his enormous strength evident though his touch was gentle.

"I'm only sorry it's taken me this long to claim you, Allesandra. I hope you'll let me stand in for my brothers and think of me as your father, as is traditional among our people."

"I have a lot to learn about your ways, but I'd really like that, Uncle Thomas." Her smile was bright, as were the feelings of belonging that were blooming in her heart.

"Call me *Tío* or just Tom, if you like. You're kin, Allesandra, and you should have been claimed a long time ago. You come to me if you need anything, and I mean anything, all right?"

Allie nodded past the lump in her throat, her eyes brimming once more. She could feel the care radiating off the man and though they'd only just met, she felt a kinship with him that could not be denied.

"The kids are away right now, but your cousins definitely want to meet you. I'll bring them by next week."

A bustling sound from the doorway drew their attention as a tall, elegant woman entered and made a beeline for them. From her coloring and the tears in her eyes, Allie guessed this was her aunt. The woman stopped before her and just stared.

"I'm Jillian." The woman's soft, cultured voice was almost musical.

"I'm Allie."

Jillian's eyes overflowed with tears as she grasped Allie gently by the forearms. "You are so beautiful, Allie. My brothers would be so proud of you. But when I look in your eyes, it's like Lilias is looking back at me."

Jillian sobbed as she dragged Allie into her arms and hugged her close. Allie felt a little overwhelmed by the emotion coming from the taller woman, but it was also a comforting feeling. Here was a woman, joined to her by blood, who had known her birth parents and loved them, and quite obviously loved her for their sake. Allie let the woman hold her as long as she wanted, finding comfort in the tight squeeze her aunt gave her.

"Jilly, let the girl breathe," Her uncle scolded cheerfully as his sister finally drew back.

"I'm just so happy you're here," Jillian said tearfully, placing a kiss on her forehead. Allie could feel the truth ring in her aunt's words.

"How are you doing?" Betina asked quietly beside her.

"I'm a little overwhelmed right now," she said softly, turning to her aunt and uncle, "but thrilled by the idea of having family."

Jillian stepped back and latched onto the arm of a tall man who'd come up behind her. "This is my mate, Ryan. Our cubs wanted to come but I thought it would be better for you to meet them tomorrow, privately, if that's okay. They can be a little overwhelming."

"How many children do you have?"

"Five at last count, and a new one on the way." Ryan patted his wife's flat tummy lovingly as he hugged her from behind. Apparently this was big news because Jillian blushed and Tom clapped his brother-in-law on the back, offering hearty congratulations.

Allie added her congratulations and stepped back as the rest of the guests crowded around to offer theirs. She found herself in a somewhat secluded corner, still flanked by those disturbing twin men who had caused such mischief earlier in the night. For the moment, Betina was chatting with Jillian and left Allie to her own devices.

"I hope you're not shy." Tim spoke softly, his attention outward, but his words directed somewhat coldly toward Allie.

"Not as a rule, no," she bristled at his implied disapproval, "but it's hard meeting family you never knew you had."

"And perhaps discovering that the world you knew isn't quite as it seemed?" Rafe gave her a teasing smile that made her feel more at ease.

"Yeah, that too," she laughed.

The sound of her amusement shot through Tim like a bolt of lightning, but he fought against the attraction he had no desire to feel. He didn't like the idea of this woman—who knew nothing of their world—coming into their lives and taking over as he had no doubt she would. Women, in his experience, always did. First they made you want them with their wiles and before you knew it, you were tied up in knots of their design.

"Stop teasing her, Rafe." He warned off his twin with a barely contained growl.

"Stop fighting the inevitable, Tim. You're only fighting fate, and that's never a good idea."

They talked over her head as if she wasn't there, but Tim was all too aware of her every movement, her every breath. She even smelled like desire and he wanted her with a sudden tightening of his body that he could do nothing to stop. When she'd kissed him on the nose in wolf form, he knew he was a goner. This little woman would seal his fate, but he wouldn't go down without a fight. That he swore.

"I'll fight whatever I damn well please." Tim growled at his twin and snarled when Allie backed away from him, straight into Rafe's arms.

He didn't like the fact that she was afraid of him and he liked even less the idea that she would accept his brother's arms around her while she ran from him. But he refused to give in to the instincts that were clamoring for him to claim her as his own. He'd never fought his twin over a woman and he refused to start now.

"You behave civilly, Tim, or I'll kick your ass myself."

Rafe's arms tightened around Allie's shoulders, pulling her back against his chest and cradling her close. Her sky blue eyes were wide with apprehension and Tim didn't like that he'd put that look on her beautiful face. Stubborn to the core though, he refused to give in and apologize. He scowled and turned away.

"Don't mind him, sweetheart," he head Rafe say, "sometimes I think he's a bear instead of a wolf, he's so snarly. Don't let him ruin your party." He heard a smacking sound and looked back to see Rafe kissing her temple, his gaze meeting his brother's with a dangerous light. "Let's get you something to drink and introduce you around. There's lots of folks here who want to meet you tonight."

With a deliberate look at his brother, Rafe tucked her little hand into the crook of his arm and led her off in the direction of the small kitchen. Tim steamed, watching after them silently when he'd like nothing better than to tackle her, drag her to the floor and fuck her brains out. But that would never do.

A few hours later Allie was completely overwhelmed. Rafe stayed by her side, introducing her around to everyone and continuing the amusing banter that kept her on her toes. Tim watched her with angry eyes that made her uncomfortable, but Rafe shot his brother some well-aimed comments that had him behaving for the most part. Betina came and went, introducing her to various people while she enjoyed the party herself, and her aunt and uncle chatted for a few minutes before taking their leave.

Aunt Jillian left early in deference to her "delicate condition", though she'd wanted to stay. Her mate, Ryan, had interceded rather forcefully on that one. The look on his face spoke volumes of the love between the two and for a short moment Allie wished, just once, a man would look at her with the eyes of love.

At about two in the morning, most of the well wishers gravitated toward the backyard. Rafe escorted her outside as the first of the guests started shifting into whatever animal with which they shared their spirit.

"It's time to run," Rafe whispered in her ear as she watched, openmouthed, as a huge man who'd been introduced to her as Rocky changed into a grizzly bear not ten yards from where she stood.

She noticed Tim taking off his shirt to her left as Rafe continued to hold her right arm politely. She wondered if they all planned to leave this way, leaving heaps of clothing in her new backyard. A small, almost hysterical giggle left her throat as she spotted Betina coming out the back door and making her way toward them.

"Are you going to, uh, run, too?" Allie felt shy asking such a question of Rafe, but he just smiled and patted her hand.

"My surly brother will lead the pack alone tonight if you want me to keep you company. I don't mind staying by your side, sweetheart."

But she could almost feel his longing to run with his twin and their pack. She could practically taste the energy coming off him in waves as he watched each new animal take to the woods. Making a decision, she released his arm and stepped back.

"You've been more than kind to me tonight, Rafe, but now it's your turn to have some fun."

"I'll keep her company until you all come back for your things, and we'll cook up some breakfast." Betina came to her rescue, facing down both brothers. "I assume the kitchen is stocked?"

Rafe laughed as Tim changed without so much as a farewell and bounded off into the woods. "Tim stocked it himself, and you know how thorough he is." Allie swore he licked his lips with an entirely different message as he held her gaze. Her blood heated and liquid fire burned between her thighs. Rafe grinned as he sniffed, almost as if he could smell her renewed arousal. "It would be kind of you to provide a little nosh for us after our run, and it'll go a long way toward making new friends."

Betina smiled archly. "Just what I was thinking. Plus, I have quite a bit to discuss with Allie, so we probably wouldn't be getting much sleep tonight anyway. We might as well do something useful while you're out gallivanting around the woods."

Rafe nodded respectfully though his eyes twinkled. He stripped off his shirt, making sure Allie caught every ripple of his hard muscled frame. He dropped his jeans and stepped out of them, toward Allie as she stood frozen. He was beautiful, a gorgeous specimen of ultra-masculine male in his prime and he was teasing her senseless. Sighing, she realized both Rafe and his unpredictable brother could make her wet with no more than a look. It was downright shameful.

Never had she wanted to stroke a hard cock the way she wanted to stroke Rafe's now, or take him in her mouth and suck the living daylights right out of him. Never had she wanted a man to possess her utterly, taking her hard, fast, and in every way imaginable. And never had she wanted such possession from two men.

Because even as surly as Tim had been all night, she was attracted to him too. She sensed the hunger riding him hard, just below the surface, and she guessed the bad mood was his way of fighting against the attraction he so obviously had no power to control. She didn't like being at the mercy of emotions she'd never experienced and never expected, so she could only imagine how hard an in-control kind of guy like Tim would find it. He was rebelling, no doubt about it, but she didn't think he'd last long. She knew for a fact she was already a goner and if, or more like *when*, these men came knocking on her bedroom door, she wouldn't be able to send either one of them away.

Rafe stood before her, gloriously nude. He changed, licking her hand with his raspy tongue before bounding away. All that was left to mark his passing was a pile of discarded clothing. Without quite realizing what she was doing, Allie bent to pick up his jeans and shirt, folding them lovingly and placing them on the nearby patio table. She did the same with Tim's discarded clothing and realized only when she caught Betina's knowing smile, she'd been caressing the soft denims the way she longed to caress their hard male flesh.

How she could be attracted to two men? Never in her life had the thought of having two men at once even entered her mind. With limited sexual experience, she hadn't even realized she could become so easily aroused, but all these two men had to do was look at her and she was theirs. It confounded her. Each of them held their own appeal, but she couldn't choose one over the other. She simply wanted both—as if that were the only right way. That thought struck her as odd, but with the new insights given her tonight at the ceremony, something echoed through her mind and told her it was the only right way for these two special beings. The only right way for her with them.

The thought shocked her. With it came the realization they would probably try to take her and possess her in the ways a man possesses a woman—but these men would do it together. Fear stiffened her limbs as she followed Betty back into the cozy house. She couldn't dwell on those two disturbing men. There were much more imperative things to discuss with Betty while she had her here.

Chapter Three

Betina and Allie talked for the remainder of the night. There was so much she had to learn, so much she had to come to terms with in such a short time. From time to time, they heard howls and roars from the forest and Allie had the sneaking suspicion the shapeshifting partygoers were having a good time on their run.

At about half past four in the morning, Betina started making breakfast. Allie was a little surprised, but followed the older woman's lead. When Betina took out three dozen eggs and began assembling enough ingredients to feed a small army, Allie started to appreciate why the older woman had started work on the feast so early. An hour and a half later, they had plates of bacon, sausage and steaks as well as mountains of fluffy eggs ready and waiting as the first of the revelers started to return.

One by one and in small groups, they entered the house, following their noses to the pleasant surprise awaiting them. Allie and Betina stood back and watched as their guests tucked in the masses of food, eating more than Allie had ever seen any human being eat in one sitting.

"We work up an appetite when we run in our fur." The deep voice at Allie's ear made her jump, though she instantly recognized Rafe's warm presence behind her. Still buttoning his shirt, he sniffed appreciatively at the food.

A moment later he was joined by Tim, whose eyes snapped fire as he looked down at Allie. Surprisingly, he seemed less angry than he'd been before and had a few scratches on his face that needed tending. She couldn't draw her eyes away from the drying blood on his cheek and before she realized quite what she was doing, she'd taken Tim by the hand and was leading him down the hall toward the small bathroom.

"Where are we going?" Tim's voice was tinged with a surprising humor she hadn't yet seen in him.

"You're hurt."

She'd been up all night and perhaps that's why she thought it should be obvious to him that if he were hurt, she would care for his injuries. It seemed perfectly logical in her tired mind, though later she would admit she hadn't been thinking clearly from the moment she saw the twins in that sacred circle the night before.

Tim tugged on her hand, slowing their progress. "I heal faster than a human. You don't have to tend me."

She looked at him as if he were crazy. "You don't want a scar do you? Or an infection? Those scratches have dirt in them, Tim."

His eyes flared as he searched her face. "So you can tell us apart. Why then are you being nice to me? I've haven't been very nice to you so far, as my brother pointed out earlier." He fingered the drying blood on his face and suddenly Allie realized the brothers had come to blows over her. The very idea caused her heart to clench in anguish and wetness to gather behind her eyes. She never wanted to come between them...at least not in a bad way.

"You're hurt," she repeated stubbornly, tugging him into the small bathroom. "I don't like to see anyone suffer needlessly." She closed the lid on the toilet and pointed. "Sit."

41

Tim actually laughed. "I'm a wolf, not a dog," he protested, but sat anyway, his gaze tracking her around the tiny room as she gathered a small washcloth and some bandages.

She ran warm water onto the small cloth and began gently bathing the long scratches on his angular face. The angry gouges started at his left temple and went down all the way to the corner of his mouth. Dirty, the nasty gashes were crusted already and had bits of what looked like tree bark and moss mixed in with the dried blood.

Tim didn't complain as she scrubbed gently at the mess on his face, and watched her every movement. Hesitating only briefly, she worked towards his firm lips, using the fingers of one hand to stretch his skin and the other to cleanse it so she could cause him the least amount of pain and still be thorough. The heat of his gaze and the warm, firm feel of his lips against her fingers began to distract her from her task.

"I haven't been very nice to you since we met, Allesandra, and I'm sorry."

Rocking back on her heels, she was more surprised by his soft tone than even his words. His expression was tender but his eyes lit with a secret fire as he took one of her small hands in his and brought it back to his mouth. Gallantly, he placed a warm kiss in the center of her palm and closing her fingers around it.

Allie shook her head. She was operating on too little sleep and everything had a fuzzy edge, but she kind of thought this man would muddle her senses no matter what. She had to clear her throat before she could talk at all.

"You don't have to apologize. I think I might understand a bit of what you were feeling. I know I've been overwhelmed more than a few times in the last few hours and have resented it." She resumed her work. Once again she had to place her fingers on his lips, but this time, he sucked them inside his mouth, swirling his tongue over her digits as she gasped.

"So you think you've got me all figured out, hmm?" His eyes sparkled as he held her wrist, placing little nibbling kisses on her fingers and knuckles.

"I didn't say that." She squirmed a little as he sucked on her thumb, letting her go with a wet popping sound as he moved up to her wrist, and then higher to the sensitive valley of her elbow.

"I need to put some ointment on your scratches, Tim."

"In a minute."

He stood, towering over her in the small space, wrapping her in his embrace. She went to him willingly, unable to deny this man anything he wanted, though she'd only just met him. She felt the rightness of his arms around her, felt the desire, the passion and the burgeoning emotions she didn't dare name. In her heart, she knew it was the beginnings of love. Whether he could love her remained to be seen, but she was fast on her way to falling head over heels in love with this man and his rakish twin, though the idea of loving two men at one time was still startling in the extreme.

Tim's firm lips drifted down, placing kisses on her shoulder, her collar bone, working toward the hollow of her throat and up her neck to her ear where he swirled his tongue briefly inside, making her shiver. He didn't stop there, biting down on her earlobe, making her yip in surprise. He moved to her temple, then her eyes, placing soft kisses on each one before tracing down in a sinuous seduction, finally capturing her lips with his in a kiss of discovery, of question and of undeniable passion.

He sought entrance and she gave in with a sigh of delight. He seduced her with every motion of his mouth, every sweep of his hands down her back, every squeeze of her ass gripped in his big palms. He began a rhythm with his tongue, echoed by the press of his hard cock against the apex of her thighs. She still wore the thin ceremonial robe, but he was clad in soft denim that molded his every bulge. And she was fast learning his bulges were very impressive indeed. Allie ran her hands over his muscular arms and wrapped her arms around his hard middle.

He was all she could have imagined and more, and he kissed like a dream. His rhythm was seductive and hypnotic, inciting all her senses as he stroked her with his whole body, making love to her with his mouth.

She felt coolness on her back as the door opened, but Tim didn't let go. Instead, a moment later she was enveloped from behind as well as in front, and she knew it was Rafe who'd entered the small room and now sandwiched her between himself and his twin.

"I came to make sure he was playing nice with you," Rafe rumbled into her ear as he swept his hands up her ribcage to her breasts and squeezed. "But I see you're getting along better than I expected. I have only one question." He tugged at the little buttons holding her robe together, freeing them one by one as Tim moved back obligingly to make room. Before she knew it, she was naked in their arms in the small bathroom. Tim's mouth moved down her neck as her breath came in harsh pants.

Rafe held her breasts in his big hands, up and ready for his brother to suck. Tim latched on to one nipple while Rafe plucked at the other with his fingers, his breath hot against her neck.

"Don't you want to hear what my question is?" Rafe prompted, making her crane her neck to try to see him.

"What?"

Rafe smiled as he bent forward to capture her lips with his. He kissed her long and hard, zeroing in on her tongue, worshipping at her lips with a hunger she'd felt only once before—from his twin. When Rafe let her up for air, it was only to allow Tim to switch over and torment her other breast with his lips, teeth and downright sinful tongue.

"I was going to ask if you planned to do this without me," Rafe teased, biting her neck with nipping teeth, "but the question is now moot."

Allie moaned as Rafe's fingers found their way to the wetness between her thighs. Big, strong fingers tangled in the neatly trimmed curls, delving within and dragging moisture back toward the back entrance that had never known a man. Allie gasped when Rafe's finger pushed down hard and was admitted with just a bit of resistance. It stung at first, but as he began a slow motion in and out of her rear, she began to feel things she never would have expected.

Tim's hands stroked downward too, his fingers plunging up her pussy with little ceremony, working in counterpoint to his brother's shallow thrusts in her virgin ass. When he dropped to his knees in front of her to suck her clit between his firm lips, she let out a little scream as she came, clenching her inner muscles hard around both of their invading fingers.

"That's it, Allie," Rafe encouraged, plunging in deeper now as she sought out his touch. "Come for us, baby. Let us show you how it will be."

Allie thrashed in their arms but neither of them let her go far. Rafe's fingers rode her ass through the maelstrom while Tim's fingers flexed and bobbed in and out of her pussy. His lips remained fastened to her clit, sucking hard as she experienced the most prolonged orgasm of her life.

And something told her these two were just getting started.

"That's enough, you three!" Betina's voice scolded them from the other side of the closed door. "Don't think we all don't know what you've been doing in there. It's not only the *were* who have good hearing. Now clean up, cool down and come out here and greet your guests, Allesandra. You can play with those boys later."

Allie's face flamed as Rafe reluctantly pulled his fingers with steady but firm pressure from her body. He swatted her butt lightly as he leaned over to retrieve her robe from the floor. Tim seemed less inclined to leave his place between her thighs, but he kissed his way up her body. He ended with a deep, passionate salute to her mouth that left her head spinning, while Rafe slid the robe up her arms and fastened it around her body.

She was powerless to dress herself, much less think, while Tim kissed her that way. When Tim let her go, finally, Rafe spun her around and clamped her into his arms, kissing her deeply while Tim watched, smoothing his hands over her back, her butt and her thighs, hiking the robe up to stroke her soft skin.

But Rafe stopped his twin, breaking the kiss and putting Allie away from them both.

"If you don't get out of here now, we won't be able to let you go. Betina's right. Go out and make friends with our people. We'll be along in a minute." He turned to the sink and began to wash his hands, but Tim stopped her by grabbing her hand.

"We're not leaving here today, Allie. We need to finish what we started."

Holding his gaze, she nodded quickly and left. She wasn't running scared exactly, but now that the heat of the moment had cooled, she wondered what she was letting herself in for.

She liked these men—no, she might actually *love* them—but it made no sense. She'd only just met them hours before, but already they'd taken up residence in her heart as if they'd always been there.

Hell, maybe they *had* always been there, just waiting for the right time to come into her life and make her yearnings real. How many times had she dreamed of a man to cherish her the way they had just done? How many times had she wished on a star for the man who would make her feel whole? And how often had she prayed for a strong man to protect and honor her, love her and make love to her?

She'd always thought it would be just one man. That's all she'd ever asked for, but the Lady apparently had other plans. They were one man. They shared the same face and the same genetics, but there were two of them. Two to pleasure, two to pleasure her and protect her. Two to make her dreams a reality.

Perhaps the Lady really knew what She was doing after all. Allie grinned at the irreverent thought as she made her way down the hall to the living room that was once again full of people.

"So do you believe me now?" Rafe asked his twin as he faced him down in the small space of the bathroom.

Tim hung his head, kneading the back of his neck. "You're so damned smug when you're right. I really hate that about you, you know?"

Rafe threw the towel he'd been using to dry his hands squarely at his brother as he grinned. "Yeah, and I hate your stubborn streak, so we're even. But you could've done some real damage to that girl if you'd kept up the cold shoulder. Can't you feel how she's joined to us already? And it's only just started!"

"Shit. I wonder what it'll be like when we're fully joined." Tim's voice was soft, speculative. "She's sweet, isn't she?" He shot his brother a look of pure masculine approval as he remembered her coming apart in their arms.

Rafe leaned back against the sink and folded his arms across his chest comfortably. "Sweeter than anything I could've imagined and she's most definitely ours."

"Damn. I didn't want to believe it, but I think you're right. There's no other way she could feel so much so soon."

"Or that we could," Rafe agreed with his twin. "She's already in my heart, Tim. She has been from almost the moment I saw her. I want to protect her, but I want to cherish her too. I've never wanted that with any woman before. She's special."

Tim had to agree, but he wasn't as comfortable talking about his feelings as his brother was. Still, this woman touched something deep inside. "It's like…like she's in my soul, somehow."

Rafe's eyes widened, obviously surprised his brother would go even that far expressing himself. "She's part of us, even now, and we can't let her go, Tim. We have to keep her safe at all costs."

Tim's expression hardened. "We won't lose her the way her sires lost her mother."

CRᴇO

"So if my sire was a *were*cat, why can't I change?" Allie asked Betina as the crowd started to disperse. They'd all shared a huge breakfast in her new home, talked over all kinds of subjects and gotten acquainted, but most were now headed home. It'd been a long, festive night, but there were things to be done with the light of day.

Betina shrugged. "Perhaps you can, but you've just never tried. Not all daughters of priestesses become priestesses themselves. For that matter, not all priestesses become the mate of a prime twin pair, and not all twins take a priestess mate. Your mother did, and had she lived to have more children, perhaps some of them would have lived quite happily with the pack. Male children of such unions are almost always fully *were*, but the females can be either *were*, magic user or both."

"Magic users?"

Betina nodded as she helped clear the dishes. "Like us, dear. Priestesses usually have to have some magic of their own in order to serve Her."

"But I don't—"

"Stop right there, Allie. You do have magic. You always have. It just hasn't been awakened fully. We started the process last night in the sacred circle. Over the next few months, you'll come more fully into your power and then it will mature with you over the years, as it has for me. We only use it in Her service, and only for good. It is the mark of the priestess that She guides our choices and helps us know when a cause is truly good, or just evil in disguise. We have an edge on other magic users because we always can see Truth."

"There are others besides priestesses who use magic?" Allie's head was spinning with even more new information. She'd thought she couldn't be surprised by anything after what she'd been through the night before, but she'd underestimated Betty.

Betina laughed her tinkling laugh. "Of course. Magic users, *were*, other shapeshifters, fey and many other kinds of magical creatures truly do exist, side by side with humanity. We keep a low profile these days, but we're still here, using our various talents and gifts for good or evil, depending on our inclinations. Since you've dedicated your life and power to the Lady, as your mother did before you, you've been blessed with Her gift of Truth. You'll find it will be your guide and aid through the rest of your development. Of all Her gifts, it is the most important to we mere mortals."

"You said 'other shapeshifters'. Are there other kinds of beings that can transform besides the *were*?"

Betina nodded solemnly. "It is a rare gift, usually given to the very blessed or the truly cursed. Great good or great evil can come of such a powerful gift. The *were*tribes carry the spirit of their totem guides with them at all times. For Tim and Rafe, it's the wolf, for your sires, it was the cougar, and so on. They can only change into the animal that shares part of their soul, but other kinds of shapeshifters can change at will into many different things. Some are limited to animals. Some can actually mimic other people, and some can even disguise themselves as inanimate objects or insubstantial things like mist or fog."

"Like those old vampire horror movies, right?" Allie was only joking, but to her surprise and chagrin, Betina was dead serious.

"It is not something I speak of often, but bloodletters do exist. They are not as common in these times as they have been in the past, but they do still walk the earth in some numbers. Beware of them. The few decent ones are never wholly good or wholly evil, but they tend to run to extremes and are hard to read. My advice is to steer clear of them. Most *were* will have nothing to do with them, but sometimes young and foolish magic users decide to play with fire and seek them out. They are ancient, Allie." Betina's eyes grew haunted. "They are as close to immortal as any being in this mortal realm can be and it has warped many of them. They do not feel emotion as we do." Betina shivered.

Allie would have asked more but Rafe sauntered into the kitchen and planted a kiss on top of her head.

"You two are awfully serious in here. Don't you think it's time you got some sleep? I mean, we're used to running wild all night but you two are just human. You need your beauty rest, right?"

Betina punched him on the arm playfully. "Watch your tongue, youngster, or I'll zap you into a toad."

Rafe gasped theatrically. "You wouldn't do that to me. Would you?"

"Don't tempt me." Betina winked. "But perhaps you're right in this one instance. I'm starting to feel the effects of our all-nighter."

"Tim thought you'd say that so he's bringing your car around. He'll drive you home, then bring Allie's car back here."

Allie perked up, hearing her name. "You've got this all planned out, don't you?"

"He's going to ransack your dresser drawers too so you'll have some clothes." He winked when she gasped. "Though you probably won't be needing them. At least not right away."

Betina leaned over to kiss Allie's cheek. "Don't let him rile you. He's a scoundrel, but he has a good heart."

The older woman left shortly thereafter and Rafe leaned back against the kitchen counter, just staring at Allie. She began to feel very uncomfortable, but tried to hold her own against his outright perusal. When he finally did speak, it wasn't anything she'd expected.

"You are so beautiful, Allesandra, inside and out." His expression softened as her insides began to melt at both the look on his face and the tone of his deep voice. "When we touched you in the ceremony, our wolves took your measure and they sat up and howled when they felt your strong spirit. They recognized their mate."

"Um...mate?" She was more than a little overwhelmed—a feeling she was beginning to get used to after the odd night she'd just spent.

Rafe watched her, his expression serious for once. "We won't rush you, but you belong to us. Just as we belong to you. You'll come to understand it and accept it in time, but for now, we need to be near you. We need to be sure you're safe at all times. Right now you're at your most vulnerable. You've been initiated, but you have much to learn and much to understand about your new role. Evil forces will stand against you and try to hurt you. It'll be our job, as your mates, to keep you safe, just as it was your sires' jobs to guard your mother. They failed." His voice was flat, but tinged with an anger he couldn't hide. "We won't. But you'll have to work with us. You'll have to get used to having us around."

Allie could hardly believe what he was saying. After knowing her only a short time, not only Rafe, but it seemed Tim as well, wanted to claim her as their mate. Betina had told her *were*wolves mated for life. In essence, the twins wanted to marry her, but unlike a regular human marriage, among *were*wolves, there really was no possibility of divorce if things didn't work out.

The thought was shocking, but it was also somehow reassuring. Allie knew little of the twins, but what she did know impressed her. They just felt *right*, somehow, when they were around her, and though she didn't understand it, she knew it instinctively. The idea of mating with the twins—mating for life in the way of their people—fired her senses.

She didn't know if she was ready to commit to any man, much less two, but she trusted Rafe when he said they wouldn't rush her. She had time yet to decide what to do about this undeniable attraction and the tempting thought of joining with them both on a permanent basis. For now though, she'd let it ride. She had things to learn and she needed to get to know the twins better to truly consider whether or not to marry them. She would see where this path led for now, trusting in the Lady to guide her steps as She had so far.

"So did you draw straws to see who got to lay down the law to me, or did you figure it would be easier coming from you rather than Tim?"

Rafe laughed out loud at her bold statement, shaking his head. "I'm ashamed to admit, it was the latter. Tim realizes he reacted badly to the idea that you were our destiny. He doesn't take orders well and he's been burned by females before. If he had his way, he'd stay the lone wolf he's become, but apparently the Lady had other plans for us. We never really expected to share a priestess mate, but we recognize the special blessing that's been given us."

"But wouldn't you rather have your own separate mates? I mean, why would you want to share?"

Rafe's smile turned wicked. "After you've joined with us, you won't ask that question. But Tim and I are closer than brothers, if that's possible to understand. We're like two halves of a whole. We're at our best when we're working together and that applies in all things." He winked at her, making her cheeks flush as she wondered just what sorts of things they might want to share with her.

Tim chose that moment to return, having made the drive into town and back in record time. Allie stood as she heard her car chugging up the slight incline of the driveway. It wasn't really suited to these roads, but she'd make do.

Rafe came up behind her, crowding her just a bit in the doorway as if he needed to be close to her.

"If you need to go anywhere besides town, we'll take you in one of our trucks. The roads up here aren't kind to city cars."

"I was just thinking my car wasn't really suited to this area, but I don't like being told what to do anymore than I suspect you do, Rafe. Next time, ask my opinion and give me advice, don't order me."

Rafe backed off, his hands held up, palms outward. "Message received, sweetheart. This whole thing is going to take some getting used to, I'm sure, but we're all running on very little sleep and excess emotion right now. I'd say it's time to grab some shut-eye before we inadvertently start World War Three."

Allie sighed as Tim bounded up the porch steps, two of her suitcases in his big hands. He'd heard what his brother said. The cautious look on his face spoke volumes. Resigned, Allie opened the screen door and he entered, a question in his eyes as he passed his brother.

"All right. You've got a point." Allie headed down the hall toward the big bedroom Betina had shown her earlier, her feet dragging, her mouth opened wide in a yawn of exhaustion. "I'll see you later."

But soft footsteps followed right behind. She heard one of the twins securing the house, but the other was dogging her steps, right up to her new bedroom door. She turned on him, surprised to see it was Tim who followed her.

"Where do you think you're going?"

Tim's expression was solemn as he looked down into her face. "Where you go, we go."

"Now wait just a minute—"

She was working up a good head of steam but Tim silenced her by dropping a light, bone-meltingly tender kiss on her lips. "For your safety," he whispered, "and our sanity, we cannot let you part from us right now. Maybe in a few months..."

"Months?" she croaked, shocked at his heart-wrenchingly honest words and the soft look in his eyes.

"Don't ask us to leave you, Allesandra. We can't. It's impossible. Our souls are already moving into alignment and after we join fully, it will be worse for a time, until we get used to it. At least that's what we've been told will happen. I tried to fight it, but there was no use. You are our mate. We'll protect you with our last breath." He stepped closer, crowding her with his large, ultra-male body. "I would die for you, Allie."

She saw the truth of his stark words written all over his face. For once, his expression wasn't shuttered against the world, and what she saw there made her breath catch.

"How can you feel so much? We only just met yesterday."

He surprised her by pulling her into his arms, caging her waist with his forearms as he looked deep into her eyes.

"My wolf knew you the moment I touched you. He sat up and howled and my blood sang. I fought it, and you'll have to forgive me for that bit of idiocy, but I can't deny it. It's part of me, just as you're becoming part of me. It's meant to be, Allie. I know you feel it too."

His impassioned words touched her heart and the look on his face melted it. "I don't understand any of this. It's crazy, but my heart knows you, Tim." Her gaze cast over his shoulder where his twin stood quietly, waiting to see what would happen. "And you, Rafe."

"You could tell us apart from the moment you met us. Do you know how rare that is? Even our own mother confuses us sometimes." Rafe smiled though she could see his pain at that admission. "Your pure heart sees us as we are—as individuals that join to form a whole. You know the differences between us when no one else can see beneath the surface. Didn't you wonder at that?"

Slowly she nodded. "I wondered why Betty couldn't tell you apart. It was obvious to me who was who." Her gaze shifted back to Tim, who still held her around the waist. "Is that true about your mother being unable to tell you apart sometimes?"

Sadness entered his eyes and she knew in her soul it was. He nodded, confirming her fear and she reached up to cup his cheek, offering what comfort she could.

"I'm so sorry."

Rafe stepped forward, reaching out and pushing them gently through the door and into the bedroom. His eyes sparkled with just a hint of humor, but she could see the fatigue in the lines of his face. They were all exhausted.

"Time for sleep," Rafe said softly, maneuvering them to the side of the huge bed.

Rafe stood behind her, Tim in front as they together stripped her bare once more. Within moments, she was naked, and only a few minutes more had both men as bare as she. Rafe picked her up by the waist and placed her gently in the center of the overly large bed. Tim shut off the light at the switch by the door, but left the small bedside lamp on, bathing the room in a soft glow. Tim took her right while Rafe settled on her left, each placing an arm around her in some way, crowding close as if they needed to touch as much of her as possible as they settled under the covers.

"Much as I'd love to ravish you at this moment," Rafe murmured in her ear as she shivered, "I'm too damned tired to do the job justice."

"And you need more time to get used to us, I think," Tim agreed, stroking her cheek, neck and one breast in a long caress. "But the time is coming, soon, when we'll join together as mates. I want to make love to you so badly, Allie. I want to lose myself in you."

She could feel both of the twins' thick cocks lying along her thighs, one in front and one behind. They were big men all over and the thought of them taking her made her shiver, but they were right. She was nervous. She needed time and some sleep to try to put this all in some kind of perspective.

"I'll come inside your sweet ass, Allie." Rafe stroked the curve of her butt and she gasped. "You have no idea how good it will feel, but I'll show you. We'll both want to take you there and we'll fuck your pussy and your ass at the same time. You'll love it. No other woman will be as well loved as you."

"I've never done that. I mean," she hesitated, whispering of her fears, "I'm afraid it will hurt."

Tim smiled into her eyes, his devilish expression reminding her just a bit of his brother. "We'll make it hurt so good. I promise, you'll enjoy every moment of it and you'll come to crave it." He leaned forward and kissed her lightly. "We would never do anything to hurt you, Allie."

"You'll learn to trust us, but we understand that trust is earned." Rafe licked her neck, making her squirm. "Starting right here and now, we'll prove you can trust us with your body...and your heart."

Tim stroked her breasts, plucking at her nipples as her head swam in sensation. "Our wolves are already loyal to you, Allie. We are yours as much as you'll be ours. Just lay back and enjoy what we can do for you. Let go and trust us just this little bit, okay?"

She could barely nod, so enflamed were her senses as Tim's hand found its way down her torso to zero in on her clit. He swept through the neatly trimmed curls above her pussy and slid his long, calloused fingers inside, seeking and finding the little button that had her clutching at his muscular arms as her eyes widened.

At that same moment, Rafe licked his finger, then moved it down and inside her back hole, just the tiniest bit, making her nearly scream, but definitely not in pain. It felt so good! She'd never realized how many nerve endings lived in that dark place, but they were all firing now and fairly screaming in pleasure as he moved slowly in and out, in smooth, small motions.

"You're nice and wet for us, Allie." Tim smiled, his eyes sparking at her in the darkness of the room as he slid his fingers out of her pussy then brought them to his lips. "And you taste like ambrosia."

Rafe nibbled gently on her ear. "I want a taste too."

His other hand roved over her front, caging her between his palms as he dipped one long finger into her channel, moving it about until she moaned breathlessly. Sliding out, he stroked back up her body and brought his glistening finger to his lips. She could see him sucking the digit that had just been inside her as his eyes closed in enjoyment. He smacked his lips as he drew back.

"Heaven," he agreed. "You taste divine, little priestess."

She couldn't believe what was happening inside her and she fairly screamed with pleasure when Tim brought his hand back down to her pussy and plunged two fingers deep inside. Coupled with Rafe's tiny penetration behind, it took only two or three long, deep strokes of Tim's fingers to bring her the most astounding orgasm of her life. She did scream then, as she came apart in their arms as she'd never come before.

Chapter Four

Just after dark, a time zone away, the vampire Dante idly examined his fingernails as a lone supplicant knelt before his ornate chair. Sighing, he touched the man's shoulder with one booted foot, jerking him upright with pain as the steel toe dug in with more force than it appeared on the surface. Dante grinned in amused boredom. Such humans as managed to find him never ceased to bring at least some minor distraction from the humdrum sameness of his endless existence.

"What do you want from me?" Dante didn't turn the force of his gaze on the human supplicant. Not yet. No, that tool would be used in time, if necessary, to gain further entertainment from the pathetic being now in front of him.

The human had the gall to stand, taking Dante by surprise. That in itself was an oddity, so he allowed the impertinence. He would see what this creature had to offer in the way of diversion before feasting on his blood and sending him on his way.

"I'm Patrick Vabian." The way the human said his name— as if Dante were supposed to recognize it—amused the ancient one.

"Congratulations. I'm sure you're very proud of that. Whoever you are." The pathetic little man actually looked ticked off, showing more spirit than Dante would have credited.

"I'm Vabian the Sorcerer," the man clarified, shooting sparks out of his hand to bounce along the far wall over Dante's shoulder. Unalarmed, but intrigued, Dante sat up straighter, eyeing the ballsy mortal with some interest.

"A magic user." Dante goaded the human, pleased by his consternation when Dante refused to be impressed. "I haven't had one of your kind come to call in many years."

"Not since Erik the Firewitch."

"Not many know of my past association with Erik." Dante let a sly smile slip over his features, twin points of pearly white fangs showing just for a moment. "We had fun burning things for a while, but eventually his own fire consumed him. Pity."

"You two did Chicago and blamed it on some old woman's cow."

Dante tensed. "Only a few beings know the truth of that time, and most of them are dead. In fact, I killed quite a few of them myself. Makes me wonder how you learned of it."

Vabian held his ground, impressing Dante slightly. "I put two and two together. Plus there are traces of your energies even today in old parts of the city. I grew up there. I recognized your power the moment I walked in here tonight."

"Very good. So in addition to your little light show, you are a Sensitive?"

Vabian nodded with stiff hauteur. "One of my many skills."

"And this interests me how?"

"Let's just say I know you've never had a love for the *were*. I have a way for you to get a little revenge on them for killing Erik and putting a stop to your fun." The human slitted his eyes in a way he probably thought made him look cunning. "Oh yes, I know it was a fight between Erik and a posse of *were* in the O'Leary's barn."

Dante eyed the man, surprised when he didn't back down from his rather over-the-top obnoxious stance.

"Bravo." Dante inspected his fingernails. "So what do I care?"

"I can give you the current lords of the *were*. On a platter."

At this Dante's interest finally piqued. "No one outside their tribes and clans knows who leads. It's a closely guarded secret."

"Not to me."

Dante sat up in his chair, more active than he had been in years. "I'm listening."

"There's a network of people who make it their business to know the doings of the *were*."

"And you would have me believe you are one of this society? A member of the *Altor Custodis*?"

"You've heard of us then?"

Dante waved his fingers in a gesture of boredom. "I've heard rumors in my day, but never have I met one who claimed to be of their number. They watch my kind as well. I always thought it prudent to steer clear of them. I've had enough beings hunting me."

"We would not hunt you." The mage had the temerity to smile. "Not if you joined with us to hunt the *were*."

Dante almost remembered what it felt like to give a damn. Almost, but not quite. It had been so long since anything had managed to make an impression on him that he felt little, if anything, for the other beings inhabiting the planet. They were transient anyway. But he alone was enduring. Cursed by his immortal existence, Dante cared little for anything other than his own comfort, and even that was sorely tested at times—like this most recent imposition by the puny human magic user.

Still, Vabian offered some diversion from his endless nights and Dante rather relished the idea of pitting himself against a pack of *were*creatures. He didn't like the *were* much. Such creatures were in fact the only beings who offered any sort of challenge to one such as he. It would be interesting to see how this human's plans played out. Plus, the *were* owed him justice. They had cost him the life of his friend. They'd killed Erik—the one human in centuries who'd gotten close to Dante. The young firewitch had been like a brother to him and his death at the hands of the *were* had been painful as well as unjustified. Oh yes, the *were* owed him justice.

For that reason, Dante would agree to lend his considerable abilities to the scheme. That and to relieve some of the incessant boredom of his existence.

Dante sighed heavily, standing from his throne. Tall and lean, he possessed a sinuous grace that had the ability to mesmerize his prey.

"All right. I'll help you, but you must provide for me in return."

Dante crooked his finger and Vabian moved forward. For the first time, Dante read fear in the human's eyes. *Good,* he thought, *the magic user was finally learning to be wary of me.*

"What do you want?" Vabian's voice was thin and reedy, laced with apprehension.

"Now what does any vampire want? Your blood, magic user. I'll help you in return for your blood."

Strictly speaking, Dante didn't need to feed from this human. He was well able to survive a few days between feedings and he'd fed only the day before, but the blood of gifted humans had an appealing quality. Magic users especially had tasty blood that fortified a vampire more than a normal human. Only *were* blood was more potent, but even over his many centuries,

Dante had only tasted *were* blood once. And that once was enough to haunt him for the remainder of his days.

Still, it was a rare thing for a magic user to fall prey to a vampire, so this opportunity was too good to pass up. Such a delicacy as Vabian's blood would be worth a little expenditure of energy on Dante's part.

Vabian stepped forward, his eyes shifty. "I agree to your terms, so long as you take only a little. I need my strength to succeed in my plan."

"But you need me for the same reason, sorcerer." Dante licked his lips as he drew ever nearer to his prey.

Vabian nodded. "I do. Which is why I'm agreeing to supply you with small amounts of my blood. Every fifth day, you may feed. I know how powerful my sorcerer's blood will make you and I know how long your kind can go between feedings."

"Well aren't you just the fount of information?" Dante sneered as he faced the shorter man. "You realize I could just take what I want and you'd be powerless to stop me."

"Not quite powerless." Vabian allowed sparks to sizzle from his fingertips in a gaudy display of power.

Dante bowed his head, though he knew the human was more prone to parlor tricks than anything that could truly hurt him. Dante had been a knight in the old days, a warrior through and through. Even a magic user was no match for him. Few were.

But he'd let the self-proclaimed sorcerer live with his delusions for now.

"I'll give you the benefit of the doubt for now."

Vabian nodded, secure in his delusion as Dante felt something like a smile lingering about his lips. It was an odd sensation, one he hadn't felt in years. The smile widened as he swooped forward to feast on the mage's bounty. Magic user blood was sweeter than wine and had more kick than tequila. He would taste it tonight for the first time in centuries. It was a rare and wonderful delicacy.

ଓଃ୭

Allie woke to a feeling of incredible warmth. In a rush, the events of the day and night before came back to her. She was a consecrated priestess-in-training now and another year older, but the most fascinating of all the new things of the past day were holding her close between them in a huge, snuggly warm bed.

Rafe and Tim.

And she was naked.

And so were they.

She knew instinctively it was Tim's warm chest that pillowed her cheek, his soft breath stirring the hair at the crown of her head. Just as she knew it was Rafe's devilish hands that rested one at her hip and one cupping between her thighs. One of her legs was thrown over Tim's thigh, his cock nestled into the groove where thigh met hip. He was warm and pulsing. And hard.

Rafe moved slightly, bringing his own hard length against the cheeks of her ass, his hand stroking lightly now over and between her folds as his dick rubbed back and forth against the softness of her butt cheeks. He was most definitely awake.

"No sense trying to fool *were* senses. We knew the moment you woke, sweetheart." Rafe's voice rumbled into her ear as he swooped close to kiss her neck with little nibbling bites and licks that made her giggle.

"Stop that. It's too early to be tickled."

"Never too early to tickle you, Allie."

Tim's sleep roughened voice came from above her head a moment before his arm swept down to the sensitive flesh of her abdomen and started making crawling motions with his big fingers. She laughed and tried to evade four suddenly attacking, giant male hands even as her mind reeled with the idea of Tim being the least bit flirtatious. Her heart broke open with the knowledge that he'd let his ever-present guard down enough to joke with her in such a foolish, carefree way.

There was no escaping their superior strength and advanced reflexes, but if she were honest with herself, she didn't really want to escape. These men did more for her long-dormant libido than any man she had even known. With only a little real experience where men were concerned, she was finding their awakening of her sexual appetites to be both frightening and titillating.

Looking down as each brother teased one of her breasts with roving fingers, she realized the titillation was both figurative and very, very literal. Suddenly the mood changed. Flirtatiousness gave way to seduction, and tickling, teasing touches turned to smooth, slow, stroking.

Allie lay back and allowed them to do what they wanted. She was too far gone to object to anything these gorgeous, caring, honorable men wanted to do to her. Sleeping in their embrace all night had softened her will and quieted her worries, though a distant voice of alarm sounded feebly in her mind. She just ignored it and luxuriated in the sexy, erotic caresses that were like none she had ever experienced before.

"Look at me, baby." Tim's voice coaxed rather than commanded as she raised her gaze to his. "Do you want this? Will you let us make love to you?"

Faced with the decision, she hesitated. "I'm a little afraid."

Rafe turned her face to his with one large hand cupping her cheek. "We'd never hurt you."

"I know." And deep in her heart, she felt the truth of that. It was her head that was frightened.

"We won't go too far. Just let us love you a little. Let us show you how it'll be when you're ready to join with us fully."

Rafe dipped his head then, licking and then sucking one of her nipples into his mouth. Allie shivered as waves of delight moved down her spine. Tim smiled rakishly at her reaction and dipped his own head to her other breast, following his twin's lead. Of course, Tim had to take things one step further, dipping one hand down her abdomen to her waist, then farther down to the apex of her thighs and the neat curls there.

As they pulled on her nipples, Tim parted her folds with one hand, and Rafe dipped one of his large fingers into her mouth. Liking the saltiness of his skin, she licked his finger and hummed with pleasure as Tim pushed one long finger up inside of her. He moved gently at first until she loosened for him, coating his fingers with her excitement.

Tim raised his head as Rafe's finger popped free of her mouth and trailed wetly down her body. Rafe let go of her nipple as the men worked in concert to shift her lightly onto her side, Tim's finger still deep within her as she faced him.

"Are you with us so far, honey?" Tim asked, looking deep into her eyes.

"I'm with you, but—"

Rafe shushed her, whispering in her ear from behind. "Easy, sweetheart. We won't hurt you."

"You keep saying that—and I believe you—but I'm still a little scared."

Tim's gaze shifted away from hers to where Rafe lay propped up on one elbow behind her. Nodding, he removed his finger from her core gently, pulling free and pausing to swirl a heated circle around the distended button at the top of her folds.

They shifted then, lifting her so that Tim sat against the wide headboard. They nestled Allie, on her back, into the wide V of Tim's thighs. Her soft hair tangled around his hard cock as her head rested on one of his powerfully muscular thighs. If she turned her head she could just about lick him, but she stayed put to see what they had in mind.

Rafe spread her legs, making her gasp. He knelt between her thighs, studying her most feminine core, and grinned. Winking, he looked up at her and moved forward, over her. His muscular arms caged her torso as he leaned down to lick his way up her abdomen to her soft breasts.

"Are you comfortable?" Tim stroked her cheeks, drawing her gaze up to his. His smile was pure deviltry and she nodded wordlessly, stunned by the position and the feel of having these two powerful men lavishing all their attention on her.

Rafe chose that moment to push two of his large fingers up into her pussy, making her gasp as her attention remained glued on Tim. He grinned devilishly as she squirmed.

"Do you want Rafe to give you more than just his fingers, sweetheart? Do you want his cock?" He gripped his own cock in one fist, his other hand cupping her cheek. "Do you want his cum?"

"How about it, Allie? Will you let us in? Will you give us the gift of your body?" Rafe's expression was as serious as she'd ever seen it when she looked down to meet his hot gaze.

How she wanted to just let it all go and let them lead her wherever they wanted. But she was still a little afraid. She wasn't a promiscuous woman and had only slept with her last two boyfriends after months of dating. She'd known these men just a short time, but already she felt closer to them than she had to either of the men in her past.

"I...I don't have a lot of experience." She could feel the blush heating her cheeks, but she knew she had to be honest with these men. "I've never done anything like this before. I mean...I've had sex, of course, but never with more than one man. At a time, I mean."

"We know, kitten." Rafe chuckled and placed a playful kiss on her tummy. "Did you think we thought you were easy?"

"Well..." She felt her blush heating even more.

Tim coaxed her gaze back up to his as Rafe moved down further, placing licking, nibbling kisses on her belly, swirling his tongue into her belly button. He moved lower, spreading her thighs wide, looping them over Tim's outstretched legs so Tim could anchor her and spread her wider, just by moving his legs.

"Only with us, Allie. We know you're only *easy* with us." A smile broke over Tim's serious features. "And we like it." He growled low in his throat as he broke eye contact with her to check his twin's progress.

Tim moved his legs apart further, taking hers wider still, and Rafe settled between them. He used his fingers and talented tongue to lick a path from bottom to top of her dripping slit. He paused to delve inside, licking, sucking and gently biting until all embarrassment was forgotten in a wave of desire that swept her right along with them wherever they would take her.

"That's it, Allie," Tim coached her softly as he watched Rafe's movements, his tongue fucking her pussy. After a moment he moved back to capture her gaze once more. She squirmed, her head moving on Tim's thigh, but his hand on her cheek kept her steady. "Are you ready for more?"

"I don't know if I can take any more!" She gasped, laughing breathlessly as Rafe drove her higher still with his tongue.

Tim smiled down at her, but the color on his high cheekbones told her of his own excitement and desire. She could see it if she moved her head just slightly, smell the musk of him with each breath she took. He smelled so good.

Holding his gaze, she daringly turned her head to the side, reaching out with her tongue to lap at the head of his hard cock. She felt his muscles tense under her body.

"Do you want it?" Tim's gaze flared as she smiled up at him and did it again, teasing him with her tongue, much as Rafe was doing to her below. "Can you take it? Will you take all of me, baby?"

"Please."

"Please what?" he prompted.

"Please, Tim. I want to taste your cum. I want your cock in my mouth. Give it to me. Please."

She didn't think he could get any hotter, but his energy sizzled around her as he guided her head into a better position on his thigh. He clenched his teeth as she took his dick into her mouth, licking, stroking and sucking as she'd never done before. Oh, she'd given head a few times, but not often, and never had she enjoyed it as much as this.

She could feel the tension and passion radiating off Tim with every stroke of her tongue and her movements fell into rhythm almost naturally with the licking Rafe was giving her below. She could only imagine the decadent picture they made on the bed. Never in her life had she dreamed she would get to live this particular naughty fantasy.

As Rafe stroked deep with fingers and tongue she came with a little cry, the excitement too much to bear. She moaned around Tim's cock and he groaned a little. A rumbling growl sounding from Rafe as he rode her through the orgasm, then stalked upward and planted his cock at the entrance of her thoroughly wet pussy.

"I'm coming inside, baby," Rafe warned in a throaty voice as the wide tip of him stretched the seldom-used passageway that needed him so badly. He growled again as he pushed further and she felt him slip deeper and deeper as he moved slowly, thoughtful of her small size compared to his huge cock.

She moaned as he seated himself fully, pushing her legs up and back with his own as he seated himself between her thighs. She had no control at all in this position and she didn't care. Never had she been filled so full, or so deep. Finally, she was complete. One hard cock in her mouth, one in her pussy, stretching her wide, sliding in deep.

Then Rafe began to move and she realized his movements pushed her mouth rhythmically up and down on his brother's cock. Tim groaned as she learned how to time her sucking licks with Rafe's motion. Then it was her turn to groan as Rafe's huge dick rubbed back and forth every time he pulled out and plunged back inside against her G spot. The man's cock was a work of art.

And she had its twin in her mouth.

The idea of it, as well as the reality of it, made her hotter than she'd ever been in her life. With a shock, she realized she was already reaching another peak. The wave of euphoria swept her up and over and still Rafe pushed, pumping in and out of her tight hole while Tim guided her head and mouth on his cock.

"Too much?" Tim asked, his voice raspy.

She shook her head no and he tensed. She did it again and would have laughed if she could at the pleasure she saw in his beautiful eyes.

"Are you with us, baby?" Rafe asked, digging in harder and faster now. She could tell from the sweat on his muscled torso and the fire in his eyes that he was close now.

She nodded and Tim's eyes glowed with satisfaction. "She's ready, Rafe. Just do her. Do her now!"

"I'm gonna come, baby. Get ready." Rafe pushed harder and harder against her tight core, so hard and unbelievably thick inside her. "Come with me, baby. Come now!"

Unbelievably, she did.

She came on command as Rafe's seed shot deep inside her, filling her repeatedly in hot spurts, warming her from the inside out. She'd never felt so full. Never had a man spent so much within her. It was sexy as hell. As was the look of sheer heaven on his face, his muscles cording, his teeth clenched.

Rafe strained and sweated above her, his handsome face reflecting the incredible pleasure he was feeling. She felt it too. She felt almost as if...as if their souls were connecting on some other plane of existence. But that had to be just fanciful thinking.

Her body continued to grind against him even as Tim pulled his thick cock from her mouth. The minute he moved away, Rafe pulled her up into his arms so he could wrap her up tight against him as the last of his seed poured from his magnificent cock.

Rafe kissed her deep and hard, cherishing her even as he came down from the same high he'd pushed her to. Never had she flown so high, so fast, or so many times in a row.

"Thank you, my love."

He kissed her tenderly and released her to lie gently back on the huge bed. She expected to meet Tim's hard thigh, but he was no longer seated behind her on the bed. She looked around and found him standing to the side looking down on them, one hand wrapped around his hard cock, stroking slowly up and down as his gaze devoured her.

Gently, Rafe pulled back from her. His cock didn't seem to want to leave, but as he pulled out with steady pressure it finally slid free. She felt so empty without him inside her!

"And thank you, brother." Rafe moved to the far side of the bed and collapsed.

"What are you thanking him for?" Allie leaned up on her elbows, wrung out but happier and more sexually satisfied than she'd ever been in her life.

Tim climbed over her, shocking her speechless as he settled between her thighs with commanding movements. He appeared to be a man on a mission and Allie wasn't about to argue. His cock was every bit as big, hard, and thick as Rafe's and she had an empty pussy that suddenly wanted it *now*.

Tim pushed home with little ceremony, his eyes closing and his head falling back as he seated himself in her slippery depths.

"He's thanking me because I agreed to let him go first." Tim began thrusting as he moved lower, his lips trailing over hers in a brief salute. His kiss deepened as he moved faster and faster, slamming home with more force than even Rafe had used in the last moments. But then, Tim was further gone—and so was she.

She grasped his shoulders, her nails digging in as he drove her to an amazingly fast and high peak, pushing her over mercilessly as he found his own release in her hot depths. He came and came, just as long, hot and hard as Rafe had, bathing her in the richness of his cum, filling her full to overflowing.

It lasted long, long minutes as he hugged her close, his muscular arms clenching her to his sweaty chest. She couldn't help but reach out with her tongue and lick him, starting another series of spurting muscle contractions inside them both.

"Baby, you're killing me!" Tim's hoarse voice scraped over her senses, firing aftershocks in her womb as he finally started to come down from the highest peak yet. "Sweet mother in heaven!"

"I hear you, brother. She's better than the best I ever had too." Rafe spoke quietly at their side and Allie looked over to find him sprawled on his back, the picture of utter satiation, his head turned and gaze riveted on them as they clung together.

Tim leaned down to kiss her sweetly, finally easing his nearly bruising grip on her smaller body. He rolled them to their sides, keeping himself nestled deep within her all the while.

"Aren't you...um..."

"No." His answer was immediate and quite definite. Tim settled her against him and shook his head as he tucked her under his chin. "Sleep, baby. Just sleep."

"But you're..."

He drew back to meet her gaze. "I'm inside you. Where I belong." Shivers raced down her spine and she clenched around him in an echo of the pleasure he'd just given her. "I intend to stay inside you as long as possible and be inside you every chance I get. You'll never know what it feels like to be without one of us in you, our cum warming you." He stroked small kisses over her temple and forehead. "Our hearts loving you."

"So that's why you let me go first." She heard Rafe's chuckle as his warm presence snuggled up behind her, one of his hands cupping her butt, caressing lightly as his semi-erect cock found a comfortable home in the crack of her ass. "Sleep now, Allie. We have lots to do today, but it can wait an hour or two while we recover. You wore us out." Rafe kissed her neck as he bit down gently on the cords of her shoulder.

How she would sleep with Tim inside her and Rafe nestled between her ass cheeks, she'd never know, but somehow it felt...right. Just as it should be. Between one moment and the next, she was fast asleep, her men wrapping her in a cocoon of warmth. And love.

Chapter Five

Allie woke sometime later, alone in the giant bed. Somehow, someone had managed to move her to a comparatively dry spot and clean up her thighs a bit. She was nowhere near as sticky as she should have been.

The very idea of one or both of the twins bathing between her legs while she was fast asleep caused a pang of strange desire to shoot through her womb. Then she remembered the details of what she'd done with them and the feeling only intensified. She'd never had such amazing sex in her whole life!

And with two men. At one time.

Somehow she couldn't work up enough outrage at the idea to be upset. Instead, she only wanted more.

Did that make her a pervert? She shrugged. It probably did, but then, there were worse things. Fucking two men at once—in the missionary position both times—hardly rated as one of the deadly sins. Did it?

And besides, she was a consecrated priestess-in-training now. The rules were different. Everyone in this new and strange world not only expected her to be with both of these guys, but encouraged it.

She got up with a sigh and searched out some clothes. Tim had indeed raided her wardrobe and brought a nice selection of things for her to wear. She did notice one sharp omission however—bras. She had to chuckle as she wondered if he'd forgotten that one vital piece of equipment on purpose.

She wasn't a buxom gal, but she did need some support or she'd be bouncing all over the place, but then, wouldn't the boys enjoy that? She'd never been much of an exhibitionist before, but suddenly she wanted to see if they'd follow the bouncing boobs with as much enthusiasm as they'd shown last night.

Choosing a loose T-shirt and jeans, she headed downstairs for breakfast, though it was the middle of the afternoon. She found Rafe and Tim in the kitchen, actually cooking. The coffee was just finishing perking in the maker and Rafe was frying bacon while Tim buttered toast. Seeing them so domestic brought a smile to her face as she paused in the doorway, but there was no sneaking up on *were*wolves. Both brothers turned as she stood there, varying smiles of male satisfaction and welcome on their handsome faces.

"We were going to make you a tray." Rafe's gaze zeroed in nicely on her breasts as she walked across the kitchen. She took the spatula from his hand to save the burning bacon.

"That's okay. It's the thought that counts." She flipped the sizzling strips, then reached up to place a gentle kiss on his lips. "Have you got a plate for the bacon? It's done."

Rafe shook his head and jumped to action. "I'll take care of it. Grab a seat and we'll all have some breakfast."

Allie smiled at the dazed expression on his face as she sauntered towards the table. A big hand shot around her waist as she passed Tim, and brought her up against his hard body. He planted a wild kiss on her lips without even pausing to let her catch her breath.

She was panting when Tim finally eased up, searching his expression for some clue to his feelings. She'd felt his desperate need for her in his kiss, his desire and his...could it be love? They'd spoken of it in passing, but no one had come out and said the actual words. Suddenly, they were what she wanted to hear most in the world.

Tim stared at her for a long moment before the wild fire in his eyes subsided. Allie was disappointed, but Rafe bustled around behind them at the table, clanging plates onto the surface and banging pots as he dumped eggs, bacon and other things on each plate.

"You're beautiful, Allie."

Tim's whisper made her catch her breath. The fire in his eyes might be banked, but it was still present, warming her. Suddenly, she was reassured.

"But a little underdressed. You forgot to pack a bra."

A wicked light entered Tim's eyes as his hands moved upwards, under the hem of her T-shirt.

"I didn't forget." When his warm hands cupped her breasts, she felt the glow of arousal reignite in her womb. "Mmm, did I tell you yet how much I love your tits?"

His use of the crude word made her womb clench. Funny, she'd never liked it when men talked dirty to her before. Apparently it had to be the right man.

"You like that?" Tim squeezed her nipples, pushing the T-shirt up farther, out of his way.

"Hey!" Rafe banged the spatula down on the table, but he was grinning from ear to ear as he watched them. "Breakfast first. We'll save that titty for later."

She shivered and Tim rubbed her nipples one last time before releasing her with a slap on her rump.

"She likes it when we talk dirty, Rafe."

"And I like the way her nipples are practically poking through that shirt."

Tim bowed his head with a grin. "Just wanted to provide an enticing view over which to enjoy our meal."

Allie tried to scold them but found herself laughing instead. "Are you going to stare at my breasts all day or eat?"

"How about we do both at the same time?" Rafe teased her, reaching out to pinch one of her hard nipples through the thin fabric of her T-shirt. She fairly jumped out of her seat, she squirmed so hard. "Take off the shirt, Allie. Let us enjoy looking at you."

"No." Allie made a show of digging into the relatively small portion of food Rafe had put on her plate.

"Aw, come on, sweetheart," Rafe wheedled as he started chomping on his own giant serving of breakfast. Tim ate quietly at her other side, but watched all with those knowing, wicked eyes of his. "Just give us a little flash."

"You saw enough before."

"Never enough," Rafe disagreed with a hot grin. "If it were up to me, I'd keep you naked all the time. Tim, can't we make a law like that or something? Females must be naked at all times when home with their mates?"

Tim chuckled. "I don't think that would go over too well with the Council, considering half of them are female."

Rafe sighed. "I guess you're right."

Allie was amazed again by how quickly these *were* could demolish a huge amount of food. She ate steadily from her much smaller plate, but still the twins finished well before her.

"No, we can't make a law about it," Tim thought over his last remaining piece of toast, "but there's no reason why we can't do our best to keep our own mate naked."

Rafe grinned as he stood. "Brilliant idea, brother." He moved behind Allie's chair as she eyed him suspiciously, but he was just too quick. His hands moved down to cup her ample breasts, rubbing the fabric of her shirt over them as the desire renewed in her quickening body.

"That shirt offends me, Rafe." Tim's stared into her eyes as he pushed back from the table. "Get rid of it."

"With pleasure." Rafe reached down and grabbed at the hem of the shirt, pulling upward. She tried to resist, but it was a half-hearted attempt at best. The look on Tim's face was scrambling her senses. He sat back, watching, as if he were the lord and master. Something about the way he gave orders was turning her on in a major way.

"Do you think her nipples are too soft?" Tim wondered, addressing his twin as if Allie weren't even there.

"I'll pinch them and see if that helps," Rafe offered, suiting words to action as he pinched her nipples hard.

"Hey!" Allie objected to the rough treatment, but was ignored as Rafe continued to play with her newly excited nipples.

"Speak only when spoken to, woman." Tim's order snapped her attention back to him. "We're the masters of your pleasure. Your place is to obey and serve our pleasure. Understood?"

What was this, she wondered, some kind of kinky game? If so, it was making her wet. She'd never been commanded in the bedroom before, but then they were in the kitchen. She'd never made love in a kitchen before either, but it looked like she was in for all kinds of new experiences with these two rascals.

"I asked, is that understood?" Tim's voice was sharper, his expression daring.

Uncertain, she nodded.

Rafe bent down over her, plucking at her nipples while he whispered in her ear. "Answer 'yes, master' when asked a direct question, woman." He bit down on her earlobe, making her gasp, but she thought she understood the dominance game they'd decided to play.

Tim stood and walked up to her as Rafe stood behind. She was still seated in the chair, between them.

"I'll have to punish you if you disobey, woman. For the last time, do you understand?"

She looked up at him, weighing her decision to go along with this game and suddenly she realized she wanted these men too badly to resist. She knew they wouldn't hurt her and they'd already shown her the greatest pleasure she'd ever known. She believed she was safe with them. Safe to explore this mysterious facet of her sexuality she hadn't known existed. Making her decision, she smiled up at Tim and watched the fire sweep full blast back into his eyes.

"Yes, master."

Rafe's fingers tightened on her nipples even as Tim stepped closer.

"Good. Now unfasten my pants." Trembling with excitement, she raised her hands to the task, finding no underwear beneath the snug denim, just all hard, ready man. "Take my cock out and put it in your mouth, woman."

She followed his commands, her own desire skyrocketing as she leaned forward to take him in her mouth. Rafe's hands slipped away and she dimly heard his zipper rasp down as she applied herself to Tim's hard cock. Soon she had him pulsing with need and it made her feel proud. She'd never been very good at giving head, or so her former boyfriends had claimed, but she'd never really wanted to do it before either.

But something about these two men—her mates, if they were to be believed—made her want to please them in every way possible. Giving them pleasure gave her pleasure as well, as if their desires were reflected back, multiplying her own.

She sucked Tim while Rafe moved around, clearing off the table. Allie was aware of his movements, but her mind was focused on Tim, her eyes watching his as she looked up. His hands were clenched in her hair, guiding her movements, but he was careful not to overwhelm her, for which she was grateful.

"Enough," Tim ordered, pulling her away from his cock by tugging on her hair. It didn't quite hurt, but his sure movements reminded her just who was in charge of this lovemaking session. "Bend over the table."

The sharp command made her realize Rafe had cleared the table completely and was now standing naked at its side.

"I think the chair would be better, brother. I want her mouth." The way Rafe looked at her nearly melted her bones. This was a man near the edge of control.

"Perhaps you're right. Over the chair, wench."

Allie tried to comply, but she didn't quite understand how they wanted her to position herself. Hesitating, she considered whether she should grab the back of the chair or place herself across the seat.

Tim's hand swatted her jeans-clad butt and she jumped. That was no love tap, but a real spank! Tim sighed as she looked back at him.

"You're still standing, wench. You're disobeying already."

"I think she needs to be taught a lesson," Rafe piped in helpfully, his voice thick with arousal.

Tim nodded at his twin. "Yeah, I think you're right." He took a seat in the chair and positioned her in front of him. "Take off the jeans." Uncertain, Allie removed her jeans hesitantly.

"And the panties." Rafe nodded toward her plain white cotton panties and she slipped them off as well. When he held out his hand, she hesitated only slightly before giving them to him. Rafe brought the panties to his nose and inhaled deeply before placing them on the table at his side.

She stood naked before the two men. Tim shimmied in his seat and worked his jeans off over his butt, pausing there to beckon to her.

"Tug these off the rest of the way, woman."

She complied, moving to crouch down in front of him and tug from the front, but he stayed her. His big hands circled her waist and turned her, guiding one leg between his so her bare ass was presented to him as she bent over his foot, tugging at his boot, and then his pant leg. She just knew he was getting an eyeful with her in this position. She could feel his gaze raking over her.

He put one finger into her folds while she bent over the other foot, shocking her upright. A stinging slap to her ass reminded her to bend over and his finger pushed deeper within, swirling through the folds of her pussy, slipping in the wet arousal these men caused just by breathing.

She had his boots and jeans off completely now, but his hand at her waist kept her in position.

"Stay right there, Allie." Rafe moved up in front of her and placed his hard cock against her lips. "You know what to do with this, right?" His wicked smile challenged her, even as Tim's long finger began to push in and out of her tight channel.

She took Rafe's cock into her mouth and licked him as he groaned. He put his hands on her head and began to thrust, just as his brother added another finger to her cunt and they started a rhythm. Impaled on both ends, Allie writhed between the two men, hotter than she'd ever been in her life.

This wasn't her! She did *not* behave this way. At least she never had before. But then, she'd never been with such magnificently sexual men before. She'd never wanted to be so wanton before, but she was fast learning to crave it. She was fast learning to crave *them*.

"Fuck! Her mouth is hot." Rafe talked above her to his twin. The idea of having them both there, talking about her while they did such outrageous things to her body made her womb clench.

"Almost as hot as her pussy," Tim agreed. "I bet her ass is even better." He paused, pulling his wet fingers from her core. "Let's try it and see."

Shockingly, Tim's wet finger moved to her anus. She tried to rise, but Rafe's strong hands on her back stayed her.

"Easy girl, he won't hurt you. He's just trying you on for size." Rafe's chuckle did little to calm her suddenly pounding heart. Her mouth was still full of Rafe's cock or she would have objected, but Rafe gave her no room to maneuver. He held her head in place on his shaft, moving shallowly in and out and giving her no choice but to obey.

She was scared and it translated in every clenched muscle in her body, but the twins apparently knew what they were doing. As Rafe soothed her with his slow, stroking motions that kept her prisoner, but gentled her at the same time, Tim moved slowly around the tight rosette, dragging moisture from her pussy to make his way easier.

With gentle motions, she felt him probing where no man but them had gone before. Incredibly, it made her hotter, but she was still afraid of what they ultimately wanted to do to her there. A finger was one thing, but these men were both very well endowed.

"Push out, Allie," Rafe whispered, bent over her body, trapping her and apparently watching every move his brother made. "He's almost in."

Tim worked his finger inside gently, stroking hidden nerve endings that made her passion rise higher. She couldn't believe how good it felt. He got her used to the possession of one finger before he drew back and added a second finger. She gasped at the momentary stretching, grabbing Rafe's hands and squeezing as he gentled her, but then her muscles accommodated him and Tim had stretched her around two of his large fingers.

It didn't hurt. Well, not much, and the pleasure was still there. And growing. The very idea that these men possessed her in every way she could imagine stirred her blood as nothing and no one ever had before.

"Oh, that's hot." Rafe growled above her as Tim's fingers slid in and out of her ass.

"Not long now," Tim agreed, though she shivered at the thought of one of their marvelous cocks taking the same path as Tim's fingers. As big as Tim's fingers were, his cock—and Rafe's—were much, much larger. The thought of it gave her pause.

Rafe surprised her by pulling back from her mouth. His dick was shiny with her saliva, hard and needy as it stood upright from his body. He lifted her slightly, bending down to kiss her lips.

"You're beautiful, Allie." His whispered words hit her heart with tender thumps. "We're going to love you like you've never been loved before. Soon."

"That's what I'm afraid of."

Rafe chuckled at her mumbled words, but Tim slapped her ass with one hand, making her clench on his invading fingers as she jumped. Masculine growls of appreciation sounded from both her mates.

"You're a disrespectful wench. Even though your eagerness for my fingers pleases me, you've still earned punishment." Tim eased his fingers from her ass and pushed her into Rafe's waiting arms as he went to the sink and washed up.

"You don't mind his little domination games, do you, Allie?" Rafe's whisper soothed her as she realized he truly cared about her response. He was her protector—even from his own brother, if need be—and he was letting her know that with every gentle touch, every soft caress.

"I wouldn't be here if I didn't want it, Rafe, but thanks for asking."

He hugged her close. "If you feel uncomfortable at all, you just tell me. Okay, honey?"

She nodded against his chest. "Don't you like a submissive woman?"

Rafe rumbled under her ear. "You know I do. I'm every bit as alpha as my brother, but only if you want it, sweetheart. Neither of us would ever hurt you. At least not in a way you didn't enjoy." He smacked her butt with an open palm, the sound echoing through the room as she squealed.

Rafe bent, kissing her senseless with Tim at her back, enclosing her in warmth. Tim's big hands rubbed up and down over her ass, the curve of her waist and then up to tangle with her hands, holding them tight behind her as Rafe stepped back.

"Yes, you're eager, but still too disobedient." He looked at her body with appraising eyes, warming her with his heated gaze.

"I bet her ass likes to be spanked," Tim tugged her closer as he bent to her ear. "Have you ever been spanked by a lover before, wench? Has your sweet ass ever turned pink under another man's hand?"

"No." She shook her head as Rafe leaned back against the table, watching her every move.

"No, what?" Tim sat on the chair and brought her over his knee.

"No, master."

"Ah, now you decide to be obedient." Tim arranged her hands downward so she was grasping the legs of the sturdy kitchen chair. "Don't think that will help you, woman. Your body is going to learn who masters it. Do you understand?"

She hesitated, momentary fear making her senses sharper. She was completely at Tim's mercy and vulnerable in this position as she'd never been in her life.

"I said, do you understand?" Tim smacked her once, lightly, on the fleshy part of her butt.

"Yes, master."

"I like the sound of that," Tim said, bringing his hand down in a harder smack, "but I'm not yet convinced."

Her breasts bobbed against the side of his thigh as Tim's spread legs supported her. His hand came down repeatedly, soft, then hard, smoothing, then smacking as she tried her best to stay still. Her position was precarious at best, but Tim held her securely with one strong hand while the other spanked her ass.

Unbelievably, the pain shifted into something hot and volatile. The strokes of his hand became tantalizing rather than torturous. He paused, spreading her legs and stroking her wet, wet pussy, even daring to smack her lightly there, sending her into orbit with an orgasm she hadn't expected.

"She likes that, Tim," Rafe commented from a few feet away. "How about you bring that pussy over here and I teach it who its master is?"

Allie gasped at the thought of it. Surely he couldn't mean...?

"You always did like to spank pussy best, didn't you?"

Tim pushed her up off his lap and placed her on the kitchen table in one smooth, powerful move. Before she knew it, she was flat on her back with Tim holding her arms above her head and Rafe between her wide-spread legs. He brought the chair over and sat, pulling her to the edge of the table so he could get an up-close-and-amazingly-personal view of her wet cunt.

"She's very wet," Rafe observed, spreading her nether lips with knowing fingers.

"She likes her discipline. That's good in a wench." Tim shifted both of her wrists to one large hand, holding her securely while his other hand zeroed in on one pouting nipple. He pinched it gently, watching it rise to his coaxing. He moved to the other nipple as Rafe suddenly plunged three huge fingers up into her sopping wet cunt.

Allie couldn't help it, she screamed. Both men had smug grins on their faces when she could again focus her eyes.

"She likes that too," Rafe observed, pulling his fingers from her still spasming pussy. "Perhaps too much."

"Seems to me she's having too much fun, Rafe. She needs a spanking to remind her of her place." Tim's voice rumbled from above her and she saw that he watched every movement his brother made between her thighs as one hand played with and pinched her nipples.

"My pleasure."

Allie tensed at the idea of what they planned to do. That had to hurt, but then, she'd been afraid of other things they'd showed her, and so far, the twins had been delightfully showing her just how wrong her assumptions had been. She tensed, but raised no objection as Rafe met her gaze with a question in his own.

"Do you want this, woman? Will you take your spanking like a dutiful wench?" Rafe asked softly, giving her a chance to cry off. Just the idea he would give her the choice made her want to follow where these two wonderful men led.

"Yes, master."

Rafe smiled wickedly as he returned his focus to her spread pussy. He played with her clit, even dipping his tongue close to lick the little nubbin, sucking it all-too-briefly into his mouth as he licked up her juices.

"You taste like warm honey," Rafe observed when he came up for air, plying his fingers deftly through her curls. "I bet all your former lovers spent hours feasting between your thighs, didn't they?" A little tug on her curls prompted an answer even as she felt her face flame.

Tim pinched one of her nipples hard, shocking her eyes up to his. "Rafe asked you a question. Did those other men enjoy licking your cum?"

She shook her head, unable to give them the embarrassing words.

Tim pressed her, concern clouding the passion flaming in his eyes. "Didn't any of your other lovers ever go down on you?" He pulled at her nipple, tugging hard while Rafe bent back to

88

her pussy, his tongue plunging deeper than she expected up her tight hole.

"No!" she cried as Rafe's tongue rasped over her sensitive tissues. "No one's ever..."

"Selfish bastards!" Tim was outraged as he lowered himself so he could kiss her deeply. When he raised his head, there were tears in her eyes which he kissed away, licking the saltiness from her skin. "We're going to kiss your pussy every morning, Allie. I promise you. It'll never want for kisses again."

The fire in Tim's eyes flamed hotter. "Maybe we'll shave you bare down there. I'd enjoy seeing you bald and I understand it'll make you even more sensitive." He seemed to think about it as his grin widened. "I'd enjoy the maintenance too, I think. What do you think, Rafe? Should we shave her?"

"Don't I get a say in this?" Allie wanted to know, forgetting her submissive role for the moment.

But that's just what her men wanted, she realized as Rafe delivered a stinging smack to her clit. She jumped in shock and roaring pleasure as the sting transformed into passion.

"You'll be shaved if we say you will. Don't forget who is master here, wench."

Rafe punctuated his words with more little slaps to different areas of her wide-spread thighs. He hit the tender crease where thigh met body, the fleshy lips framing the tender hole. He smacked the pad at the top and all around the sensitive nubbin that stood out, practically screaming for his attention, but avoided that most tender part until the last stinging blow.

When he smacked her clit once more, she came like a rocket, her body spasming as Rafe rubbed her with circular motions, milking the orgasm for all it was worth. She cried out as Tim pinched her nipples, sucking one deep into his mouth, using his teeth gently on her excited skin, while her orgasm raged on and on.

Even before she came down from the sky, she felt herself being lifted from the table and bent over the edge, face down. Rafe pushed the hard head of his rampant cock against her until her pussy swallowed it down where it belonged. At the same time, Tim moved in front of her, pressing his cock to her mouth.

She sucked at him eagerly as Rafe drove into her. There was no respite. The amazingly high plateau she'd reached with that last orgasm stretched on and on as her men pushed her still higher. Rafe pounded into her from behind, pushing her mouth onto Tim's cock in a driving rhythm. She strained toward the higher peak, feeling something amazing lay just out of reach, but Rafe and Tim were there, with her, pushing her pleasure higher than it had ever gone before.

"I'm close," Rafe said over her head as Tim grunted in agreement.

"Come for us now, baby," Tim coaxed with a growl as Rafe brought his big hand down once, twice, three times on her ass.

Allie splintered apart with a keening cry as she soared even higher than before. She felt Rafe tense inside her and felt the spurts of hot cum fill her womb, then her mouth as Tim joined him in orgasm, gushing inside her mouth. He tried to move away, but she held him, sucking hard at his spasming cock, drinking down his cum as if it were the finest wine.

And to her it was. He tasted divine. Of heaven and love. He tasted like he was hers, like she belonged to him and his cum belonged to her. She would never get enough.

"God, baby!" Tim choked out, watching her as she looked up at him through her eyelashes, licking every last drop into her mouth. Suddenly she wanted to taste Rafe, but he was still coming inside her.

Rafe pulled gently out long moments later and she turned in his arms. Smiling devilishly, she leaned down to suck his cock into her mouth, humming in satisfaction when he gasped.

"Baby, you're killing me!" Rafe gasped as his cock tried to come back to life under her mouth.

She smiled as she pulled away. "I like the taste of your brother. I just wanted to taste you too, Rafe."

Both men groaned at her admission.

"She's definitely going to be the death of us," Tim said as he collapsed against the table. Rafe fell into the chair and pulled her down onto his lap as he grinned over at his twin.

"Yeah, but what a way to go."

Chapter Six

Her Aunt Jilly's kids were as rambunctious and joyful as a sackful of kittens. Allie found herself just sitting back and watching later that evening as the younger ones careened around her new living room. The place was kid-proof enough that they could chase each other without the adults having to intervene too much, but other than being very active, they were quiet children.

Allie thought that might have something to do with the fact that they were *were*cats, but she'd have to ask Rafe or Tim later to be sure.

"Don't mind the cubs, they have a lot of energy at their age."

Ryan smiled as he scooped the five-year-old off the floor, patted him on the butt and sent him back to where the seven- and eight-year-olds were stalking each other around the ottoman. Allie instinctively liked the older man, finding him steady of character and blessed with a wry wit. He seemed to act as a calming influence on the spirited children and his wife as well.

Allie simply loved the way her Aunt Jilly bubbled. She had an effervescent personality that made you just want to be near her.

"Do they... I mean, can they...um...change?"

"Shift, you mean?" Jilly laughed as she shook her head. "No, not for a few years yet, thank goodness. They're hard enough to keep track of as it is!"

Allie laughed with them but realized how much she didn't know about her heritage. Unfamiliar with children of any species, Allie admitted freely that she was more than a bit overwhelmed by the brood her aunt and uncle managed with calm aplomb.

"Of course, Leslie will be beginning her training next year." Ryan patted his oldest child's head. The girl had flowing golden hair and wide golden topaz eyes. She was eleven now, which meant this mysterious "training", which Allie supposed had something to do with learning how to shift into animal form, would start around age twelve.

Allie didn't quite understand the mixed look of pride and concern in Ryan and Jilly's eyes as they looked at their oldest, but she wondered if learning how to shift wasn't more dangerous than it appeared. Yet another thing she'd have to ask Rafe and Tim when she had a chance. Suddenly the list of things she needed to learn seemed very long.

Rafe collapsed onto the couch next to her and wrapped one big arm around her shoulders, drawing Allie against his side. Rafe and Tim had volunteered to load the dishwasher after dinner while Allie visited with her aunt and uncle and their cubs.

"The Cougar Clan allows their cubs to shift beginning at thirteen. Some of the other tribes, packs and clans set different ages, but most coincide with the onset of puberty." Rafe's deep voice sounded low in her ear as he explained.

"How did you know?"

Rafe kissed the tip of her nose before moving back. "Sweetheart, the questions in your eyes were plain to see."

Allie looked over at her family, only to intercept a knowing nod between her aunt and uncle. She thought she knew them, and their senses of humor, well enough by now to call them on it.

"Now what was that for?" she challenged the older couple.

Jilly laughed while Ryan winked at her. "It's just good to see our Rafe mated, that's all. Some thought this day would never come—especially all his ex-girlfriends." Ryan laughed outright at that and Allie turned mildly accusing eyes to Rafe.

"Are you a playboy, Rafe? And how in the world do they know if we're mated or not?"

Jilly leaned forward with a conspiratorial grin. "As to the first, yes, Rafe has broken many a wolf bitch's heart. And as for the latter, their scent is all over you, as is yours on them. Add to that the way he can practically read your mind already, and well, I've seen enough true matings in my time to know when I'm in the presence of the real thing. You three were meant to be, and I couldn't be happier for you." Jilly grabbed her hands and squeezed, her enthusiasm spilling over even as Allie blushed fiercely.

Allie sniffed at her hands when Jilly released her, inviting them to giggle at her antics. "What I want to know is, if I'm half *were*cat, how come I don't have such sharp senses?"

"Ah," Tim sat down on her other side and grabbed her hand, bringing it to his lips for a smacking kiss, "but your mother was a priestess. You may not have all that much of the cougar in you—which is a good thing when you consider you're mated to wolves—but you more than make up for it in other ways, sweetheart."

Jillian rose and plunked the two-year-old down on Allie's unsuspecting lap. "Hold Janice for a minute while I take a potty break, okay?"

Without waiting for an answer, Jilly took off down the hall, leaving Allie with a squirming baby on her lap and three grown men smirking at her. Allie hadn't been around a lot of little kids in her time and was a little afraid of the tiny, rambunctious thing crawling around on her lap. She put her arms out reflexively when the baby tipped back to smile up at her and nearly toppled off her knees.

Rafe and Tim were there too—one of each of their big hands moving like lightning to bracket hers and save the oblivious baby girl from a tumble.

"She's a handful," Allie commented to Ryan, though the baby's father seemed occupied in chasing down the seven-year-old, an energetic little boy named Harry.

"You're doing fine," Rafe crooned near her ear, letting the baby grab one of his big fingers as she cooed up at him. She was a charmer, there was no doubt of that, with her happy golden eyes and wispy blonde curls.

"I'm not used to babies."

"Yeah," Rafe chuckled near her ear, "I sort of figured that out. Don't worry, you're a natural."

Baby Janice decided to travel, crawling haphazardly across Allie's lap to pin herself to Tim's chest. Allie laughed, thinking Tim wouldn't know how to handle the little girl, but he amazed her with the natural way he sheltered the little munchkin in his arms. He was so good with her, so loving and attentive and completely unconcerned that the little girl seemed to want to drool all over his shirt.

Hell, Allie thought with a chuckle, she knew how the little chick felt! Tim's chest was indeed drool-worthy and even the younger generation seemed to appreciate it.

A small towel pitched through the air and before Allie even realized what exactly it was, Tim's hand shot up and caught it, sweeping it under the little wet chin against his chest. Those *were* reflexes were really something.

"Thanks, Ry."

Ryan winked as he settled back in his chair, the five-year-old now on his lap, blinking sleepily.

"No problem. She hasn't grown out of the drooling thing yet. Hopefully soon."

"But before long you'll have a new little drooler, won't you?" Rafe asked.

Allie watched the almost envious light in Rafe's eyes as he watched the kids all around and wondered if he was thinking of starting a family with her. They hadn't discussed anything, but then, they hadn't used any protection that morning either.

The idea of children awed her. Allie hadn't really thought about having kids. She'd always thought she'd have to find a man who could put up with her before she even thought about reproducing, but that problem had been amply solved. She hadn't found just one man who wanted her, but two!

Now the thoughts of having their babies had serious traction. Allie watched the way Tim cradled the happy, sleepy toddler, realizing he'd be a great father. The look in Rafe's eyes spoke eloquently of his hunger for a child too, but there was still one major problem. How would they know exactly whose baby she was having, if she managed to get pregnant?

A DNA test wouldn't work because these two were identical twins—even if they wanted to subject their *were* DNA to testing. She had to guess they didn't want any regular lab getting their hands on what was probably some very non-standard DNA. Rafe tugged her closer, placing a kiss on the crown of her head.

"Don't think so hard, Allie. We have time yet to answer all your questions."

That shocked her gaze up to his. "You are reading my mind, aren't you?"

Rafe shrugged. "Not really. Not completely. But your expressions are open to me. I'm learning you, Allie, just as you're learning me."

"Rafe, I don't have a clue about you!" She laughed up at him, floored by the tender teasing in his expression.

"Oh, no?" He tugged her even closer and bent to whisper in her ear. "I bet you can tell what I'm thinking about right now."

The hot, wet tongue swiping a seductive path around her earlobe gave her the first clue. He bit down gently but with enough force to make her take notice.

"Behave, Rafe! We have company."

"Don't mind us." Jilly swept into the room like whirlwind and sat back down across from Allie. "We were young and newly mated once ourselves." She clasped her mate's hand across the distance between their two chairs and the look they shared was so tender, so loving, it touched Allie's soft heart.

"The early days are good," Ryan said softly, still holding his wife's eyes, "but a true mating only grows better with time." He looked over at Rafe, Allie, and Tim who now cradled a sleeping baby Janice on his chest. "You three should start thinking about a family."

Allie nearly choked, inhaling down the wrong pipe as Rafe thumped her on the back and laughed. She felt her cheeks flushing with bright red heat as all attention focused in on her. Surprisingly it was Tim who came to her defense.

"There's time for that discussion yet, Ry. This is all still very new to Allie." His softly pitched voice washed over her senses and the look she caught in his eyes melted her heart. Tim might be a bit gruff on the exterior, but he was gentle when it counted. He knew how to care for little things and he didn't

97

mind the mess the baby made of his shirt. For that alone, she loved him.

Love?

Now where had that thought come from? Allie sat back and let the conversation flow around her as the realization set in. She loved Tim. And Rafe. How it had happened, or exactly when, she still didn't know, but it was there all the same—the fragile kernel of love, just beginning to sprout.

Oh, there was a lot more to it, she knew, but it was a beginning. These two incredible men had somehow wiggled their way into her heart and the seed they'd planted there was beginning to grow. A fragile thing now, she knew if given half a chance, it could bloom into something magnificent.

The question was, dare she let it grow and find out?

So much was at risk—her heart, her life plan, even her sanity. What if they didn't love her back? She knew that would destroy her and a sudden fear settled in the pit of her stomach.

Rafe's warm hand tunneled under her hair to cup the back of her neck.

"You okay, sweetheart?"

Allie put away her troubling thoughts and tried to smile for him, but she knew it failed to convince him.

"Sure." She allowed him to tug her closer until her cheek rested against his shoulder.

"I keep forgetting that though you may look like your daddies, you don't have *were* stamina." Her aunt Jillian's voice was gentle as were the golden eyes turned on her when she looked over at the older woman. "We have all the time in the world now to get to know each other and be a family." Jillian stood and took Allie's hands in hers, tugging her upwards into a warm hug. "I'm so glad you're back with us, my dear. So glad you've finally come home."

Ryan and the twins stood too, gathering the kids' belongings and settling the sleepy younger ones into various carriers and coats. Inside of a half-hour, the entire family was packed up and on their way home, leaving Allie alone once more with her two new mates.

"Are you really tired?" Rafe asked with a wicked gleam in his eyes.

Tim was unbuttoning his shirt, but Allie figured it was because he wanted to change out of the baby drool. Then he started shucking his jeans and Allie's eyes widened.

"No, not really." She hedged. "Why?"

"We have a few things to show you, Allie. Things you need to learn about being *were*, and things you need to understand before you begin to test the limits of your new and evolving powers."

Tim was all seriousness as he stood before her now, naked and without a hint of self-consciousness. Then again, with a body like that he probably never would have a reason to feel self-conscious. Nope, no reason at all.

"Okay..." She jumped when Rafe came up silently behind her, pulling her back against his chest. "What exactly did you have in mind?"

"Big brother is going to demonstrate the various stages of the change for you. It's not something we like to do often, but when needed, a partial shift can be very useful."

"You mean you can do the wolfman thing from the movies?" She couldn't help but tease a little as Rafe rocked her back against his chest. "And why did you call him 'big brother'? Aren't you twins?"

"Well, Tim was born first by a few minutes, so he's just slightly older. And to answer your rather disrespectful question—yes, a half-shift can leave us standing upright while giving us the benefit of claws and teeth."

"It can also vastly increase our strength." Tim picked up the narrative as he stretched his limbs in preparation. "It's all a matter of degrees, but it's not easy to hold a partial shift and it consumes a lot of energy. We don't do it lightly, but you need to see it."

Allie sobered up immediately. "I don't want you to do it if it will cause you pain, Tim. I can take your word on it."

Tim paused as if surprised, then shrugged. "No, you need to see this. I don't want you being afraid of us if we need to do this someday in an emergency situation. You need to know what to expect."

She would have objected more, but the look on Tim's face, along with the tightening of Rafe's arms around her warned her not to push further. Instead she settled back against Rafe and waited for the show.

She didn't have to wait long. Tim started to shift, as she'd seen before, but this time it was slower, much more deliberate. It was beautiful in a grotesque sort of way as she watched his bones reshaping themselves and his handsome face distort into an elongated snout that wasn't quite wolf and not quite human either. It was a mix of the two and Tim was right—it scared the crap out of her.

But Allie was a strong woman and having Rafe's arms around her helped. As did the power spiking through her newly awakened magical senses. She steeled her spine as Tim stalked forward on legs that moved differently than normal human legs. When he put his snout right in her face menacingly, she fought the urge to shut her eyes and turn away. This was Tim! She'd seen him change into this sinister form not minutes before. Why then couldn't she control the fear?

"It's all right, Allie. What you're feeling is part of our power. In the half-shift, we can use our abilities to project fear into our opponents, but it isn't very exact. We can't direct it to specific people—only in general. So if we're ever in a situation where we half-shift to protect you, some of this projection might spill over to you."

"You need to know what it feels like so you can recognize it and learn to shield it out." Tim's voice was closer to a growl through the larger teeth, his words slurred slightly and in a deeper tone, but he could still talk, which amazed her. Allie tried to erect a mental wall between herself and the feelings of fear bombarding her. Now that she knew what to look for, it was relatively easy to recognize the manipulation of her feelings.

She tugged against Rafe's hold and he cautiously let her go, one inch at a time. Steeling herself, she touched Tim's shaggy face, marveling at the change in the man she knew. It was the eyes that finally settled her nerves. Those were Tim's eyes. Not the eyes of a beast.

She stepped closer and lowered her hands to his muscular shoulders as she learned the new shape and feel of him. Daring greatly, she wondered how it would feel to hug him. She stepped closer and tried it out, shocking him, she could tell, from the way his arms hesitated before closing around her.

"It's okay. I'm not scared anymore."

The brothers looked at each other over the head of their petite mate and Tim's eyes reflected Rafe's own astonishment.

"You're a miracle," Rafe whispered, watching Allie settle into the arms of the beast that was his brother.

After a short time, she let go of Tim, stepping back, deliberately taking in the full view of the man-monster. Her head tilted as her eyes narrowed.

"Does it hurt?"

Tim nodded slightly. "It's bearable for short periods."

"But the change wants to complete. Either wolf or human. We weren't designed to hold the line between the two for long." Rafe stepped up next to her and tucked her under his arm. She was such a precious thing.

"Then let it complete, Tim. I don't want to see you in pain."

Tim growled softly as he worked the roped muscles in his shoulders. With a sigh, he let the change go until he stood before them once more in fully human form. The lines of strain were evident on his face as he bent to pick up his pants and began to tug them on.

Rafe stroked her arm, feeling her distress. "We practice holding the half-form, Allie. It hurts and it's hard to control, but it can also be very useful."

"In what way?"

"We're stronger in that form than we are in any other." Even Tim's voice sounded weary.

"We have the heightened senses of a wolf and the dexterity of a human. We also have nearly double the strength than we have in either form."

"Amazing."

"Glad you think so." The twinkle in Tim's weary eyes warmed her. He was so different at times from his twin, yet he had the same dry wit Rafe showed in abundance. It was just better hidden.

"About what Ryan said before…" Allie seemed to want to say something but the enchanting flush on her rosy cheeks told

Rafe she was embarrassed. He thought back to what the *were*cat had been talking about that might make her blush so prettily.

"You mean about us having children?"

Allie nodded. "How—um, how would we know whose it is?"

Tim stepped right up to her, cupping her face so she would meet his eyes. "Would it matter so much, Allie? Rafe and I are identical in every way. You're the only person who can really even tell us apart."

"You may look the same on the outside, but inside, where it counts," her voice was surprisingly impassioned, "you're two separate individuals, each unique and special. But the identical twin thing would make it really hard to tell—even scientifically—which of you fathered any children we might have."

Rafe sighed, stroking her shoulder. "Don't you think we've thought about that?"

She looked up at him and his breath caught in his chest. The light in her eyes, the way she could tell who was who was unique in their world. She was unique.

"And?" she prompted him.

Rafe had to scramble for the thread of the conversation. Her beauty sidetracked him every time. Luckily Tim was there to complete his thoughts—as they often did for one another. They were a team from the moment they'd been conceived and would always be.

"And though it would be nice to know, we don't see how it's possible. We have one last person we could ask, but if Betina doesn't see a way, then we'll just have to live with it."

Rafe stroked her arm. "It wouldn't be so bad really. Any children we have will be all of ours. We'll all raise them and love them all the same regardless of which sperm did the job."

"You guys are amazing." Allie shook her head with a soft smile that enchanted Rafe so much he had to lean down and kiss her.

"No, Allie, you're the amazing one."

CR80

Rafe and Tim spent the remainder of the evening going over the history of the *were*, explaining the various tribes, packs and clans, though it was a great deal of information for anyone to take in at one time. Rafe admired the way Allie tried to keep it all straight in her mind and the innocent way she blinked at some of their explanations. She was worming her way deeper and deeper into his heart with every move, every gesture.

"There are various kinds of supernaturals," Tim was saying "*Were*folk are only one of many."

"Betty mentioned something about, um, vampires?" Allie's voice lifted in question as if she couldn't quite believe she was having this conversation. Rafe had to chuckle, though Tim treated her question with all seriousness.

"Bloodletters," he spat the word. "They don't mix with our kind. Actually, few of the supernatural races mix well with others. Even all *were*folk don't quite get along. There are the natural oppositions of canine and cat, predator and prey, but for the most part we can overcome our animal natures to deal well enough with one another. We understand each other to some extent, the difficulties and challenges of being *were*, which is not something that can be said for the other races."

"Who could possibly understand a bloodletter?" Rafe added. "I mean, some of those folks are downright ancient. They originated in different times, with different customs and I can only imagine the things they've seen and done over their centuries. Although *were*folk do live longer than humans, we're not as close to immortal as they are. It puts a wedge between them and any other folk—except perhaps the fey."

"You mean like fairies?" Allie giggled. "Who knew Tinkerbell was real?"

"The few I've seen don't care for the Disney analogy, Allie, so if you ever have a run-in with any of the fey, be careful about mentioning that sort of thing."

"Why? What could they do to me?"

"Good question." Tim sat back in his chair. "The fey have enormous power in their own realm. Their powers are somewhat limited here in our world, but still quite formidable. They use magic with almost cavalier abandon since it never seems to drain them. Not like with human magic users."

"Magic is their domain," Rafe said thoughtfully. "They could transport you to their realm, drag you Underhill where time passes in strange ways. When they finally let you go, everything you know could have changed, everyone you knew could be gone. Or a really angry and malicious fey could transform you into something, hex you or curse you. All in all, it's better to steer clear of them and if you do cross paths with one, treat them with extra respect."

Allie nodded solemnly, her eyes so wide, Rafe just had to lean down and kiss her on the nose. She was so beautiful, she stole his breath and brought out his mischievous side.

"Now as for magic users, mages, witches, warlocks, sorcerers and the like—"

She held up a hand. "Let me guess, you steer clear of them too."

"Nobody likes a smart ass, Allie," Rafe grinned at her, "but yes, human mages are just as unpredictable as the rest, though there are a few—like you, for example—who are utterly trustworthy."

"Those few who have dedicated their lives and their power to the service of the Lady are our allies and we have vowed to protect them," Tim added. "Almost all *were,* with few exceptions, adhere to this pact, though it wasn't always so. Betina forged the alliance and she's the one who's helped keep it strong, even after the devastating loss of your mother and her mates."

"When your mother was murdered, our people lost their leaders as well. The tribes, packs and clans were thrown into turmoil for a time until Tim and I could establish ourselves. We were fourteen at the time, so it was a tough fight. We'd only just learned to shift the year before and weren't comfortable in our skins yet."

"We had to fight a lot in those early days to establish our place. Allie," Tim's voice grew even more somber. "I know *were* customs can seem brutal to humans, but when our authority is challenged, we have to face all threats. Most often that means a fight, sometimes a fight to the death. When such things happen, you can't interfere or object, no matter how much you might want to."

"But that's barbaric!"

Rafe sighed. "It's *were* law. Tim and I are the leaders of all *were* on this continent. Our word is law, but even we are not above the law. The laws have been passed down through generations to us and we're left with them to uphold and see carried out. There aren't many and they aren't complex, but one of the most sacred is the right of challenge. It's part of our very natures to fight to settle disputes and only the strongest of us can lead. For this generation, that's Tim and me. We've proven it time and again, and we'll continue to prove it when some fool is stupid enough to challenge us."

He saw her eyes widen at his vehement response but she had to know the truth. She had to understand the way it was for them. They were *were*wolves first, lords of all *were* for their generation, and the safety of the *were* and the continuation of their various species had to take precedence over her more human sensibilities.

This was one time when her being raised away from her people was a true detriment. She didn't understand their ways, even though she was half-*were* herself. Even if she couldn't shift, she had the instincts of her sires somewhere buried deep down inside, Rafe would bet his life on it.

"I think that's enough for tonight," Tim said around a yawn. "We have time yet to tackle all of this. Betina is coming in the morning and she'll begin working with you on harnessing your magic."

Tim stood and shrugged out of his shirt. Rafe knew he had to do the same. Where his brother went, he had to go as well. They'd discussed this earlier while they were in the kitchen after dinner. They'd agreed they needed to put a little bit of space between themselves and Allie, just for a short time.

Both of them had seen the fear in her eyes when she thought they weren't looking. Both of them had seen the questions, the distraught expressions that passed over her features when she thought of them together. She needed time, they decided, to come to terms with this new relationship, and they vowed to give her as much time as they could.

Rafe stood and shucked his clothing, laying it regretfully on the couch.

"Where are you going?"

"Not far, sweetheart," Rafe assured her though his heart felt a pang of longing as he stroked his hand down her soft arm. "We'll be near if you need us, but we have to go out tonight."

The brothers had also agreed not to tell her of this particular plan. She didn't need to know why they were stepping back, it would only embarrass or perhaps anger her. No, she just needed some time and they would give it to her.

"Will you be back before morning at least?"

Rafe sighed as he moved toward the back patio doors with his brother. "We'll try. But don't be afraid. If you need us, just call. We'll be nearby."

He could see the questions in her beautiful eyes, but couldn't face them. With a quick kiss, he left her standing near the door as he padded out after Tim. He sought the change quickly before he gave in to selfish desire and went back to her. This was for the best, he knew. She needed space, and space was what he would give her, even though he wanted nothing more than to sink between her luscious thighs and stay inside her for the rest of his life.

CR80

After a long night spent tossing and turning, Allie awoke to the smell of bacon and coffee. Tim and Rafe had been busy, leaving a tray of steaming food on the table at the side of the bed, but neither of them were anywhere to be seen.

Breakfasting in bed made her feel decadent and cherished, as did the small bouquet of wildflowers in a little vase on one corner of the tray. She recognized some of the herbal flowers from the nearby forest, but some were foreign to her. All were enchanting, as was the thought of her two strong men picking them with their big hands for her.

"Ah, sleeping beauty awakes." Rafe winked at her from the doorway, looking altogether too sexy for this early in the morning. "Betina is waiting for you downstairs whenever you're ready."

"What time is it?" It couldn't be that late yet, could it?

Rafe chuckled as she scrambled for her watch on the nightstand. "It's after ten, sweetheart. You looked so peaceful, we didn't have the heart to wake you."

"Oh my gosh! I haven't slept this late in years."

"It's been an eventful few days."

Rafe came over and took the now-empty tray off her lap. "Why don't you grab a shower? Betina can wait a few more minutes. She said she's going to be working with you all day and asked Tim and I to vamoose. Something about masculine energy interfering with her magic. I didn't follow it all myself."

She leaned up and kissed him, unable to resist, but he moved back after only a quick peck.

"You've got to get moving. I promised I'd get you up, not waylay you."

He stood and she followed suit, yelping when he swatted her ass on the way to the attached bathroom as he took the tray out into the hall.

The men were gone by the time Allie made her way downstairs, but the scent of coffee lingered. She filled her mug before meeting Betina in the living room with a slightly embarrassed smile.

"Sorry, I overslept."

"Not to worry, dear. I bet those boys tired you out."

"I wish," Allie muttered into her coffee cup as Betina laughed.

"Don't let them bedevil you. They're good boys, but they can be a handful."

Allie chose not to comment and after a few preliminaries, Betina got down to the serious work of the day. That work proved to be teaching Allie about magical shielding. It all sounded so foreign at first, but after a while Allie began to sense the energies Betty talked about and was able to direct them in subtle ways as Betty coached her.

It wasn't much, but it was a start, and Betina seemed pleased at the end of the long day when she said Allie was able to put up at least a rudimentary shield, which was apparently an important thing. Betina left her with homework too. She was to practice putting up and taking down the shield energies in ever larger spherical shapes around herself and around objects. She had to try to do it quickly. To call upon the energy fast and redirect it even faster. It was hard, tiring work, but Betty's praise seemed to make it all worthwhile.

Chapter Seven

Travel was always tedious for one of his kind, but it had become much more simplified now that Dante had his own airplane. The technology of the modern world had it hands down over the slower methods of the past. As long as he had enough money, a vampire could manage very well in this modern world. A pilot's license didn't hurt either.

Dante had been feeding off the magic user for a few weeks now, enjoying the little charge the magicked blood gave him. He'd fed from the dregs of humanity for too long—the inconsolable, the unhappy and those who searched endlessly for meaning in their limited existence. Such were the inhabitants of the bars and clubs he'd been trolling for the past few decades, and he realized only now, with fresh magic user blood flowing in him, he'd become as desolate and barren in his endless existence as those poor mortals he preyed upon.

Truly, you are what you eat.

He felt energized to a new degree, able to work up resentment again at the unfair way the *were* had interfered with Erik's path. Erik had been a young warlock, just testing his gift for firestarting. If truth be told, Dante had gravitated toward Erik simply because he looked so much like his long-dead younger brother, Elian. Both Elian and Erik shared that same devil-may-care smile and lust for living that Dante believed had died within him the day he was transformed into the immortal being he was now.

Erik was only testing his powers, a successful young blacksmith living in nineteenth century Chicago. He used his firestarting gift in his work as a blacksmith, able to heat iron with nothing but his magic gift. His work was good, his muscles strong, like Elian's had been from wielding a sword from a young age. The look of the two men, born centuries apart and on different continents, was eerily similar as well. Both had the longish, dark hair, sparkling blue eyes and roguish grin Dante remembered nostalgically to this very day.

When Dante's horse threw a shoe, he'd found Erik the blacksmith quite by accident and had been struck dumb by the firewitch's uncanny resemblance to Elian. Erik, in addition to being a gifted blacksmith and a budding firewitch, also had a certain sensitivity. He could tell Dante wasn't quite the foreign traveler he seemed and was wary at first, asking questions most mortals wouldn't dare put to a centuries-old vampire. But Erik was fearless. Much as Elian had been.

After some initial distrust, Erik had proven himself by saving Dante's life. He'd provided a safe hiding place when Dante had been caught out too close to dawn. Erik could have killed him easily that day, but he didn't. He'd proven himself a friend and in subsequent days, Dante enjoyed helping the young firewitch test the bounds of his powers, much as he had helped Elian perfect his fighting skills. For the first time in centuries, Dante felt like he had something of his brother back, if only for a short time.

Erik didn't like the *were*. His hatred of them ran deep because the local wolf pack that lived just outside of town was led by a murderous son of a bitch who had killed a young girl Erik was sweet on years before. It had been that good for nothing *were*wolf who had roused the lords of the *were* against him, ending Erik's young life.

But Erik went down fighting. It was his acts of self-defense against a large contingent of *were*folk that started the Great Chicago Fire on October 8, 1871.

Given the dry summer and the inadequacies of fire fighting at that time, the fire quickly spread. Dante supposed in hindsight he could have done something to stop it at its inception, but when he arrived at the scene too late—too damned late to save Erik from being torn to pieces by the *were*—he didn't care. He wanted them to burn. He wanted them all to burn for killing his friend, his little brother, all over again.

Tormented by grief, Dante let the fire go unchecked. He had no way of knowing it would destroy so much, but in those nights that followed Erik's death, he was too numb to care. Only years later did he feel the guilt. Guilt first for not being there to save Erik from being hunted by those curs and then there was the guilt he could never quite acknowledge for allowing so much of a city he had called home to burn. So many people were injured by the fire, both physically and mentally. He fled Chicago not long after and had never returned.

Now there was another young magic user in his life, but this one in no way reminded him of his little brother. No, Vabian was as vain and self-centered as any mortal, and twice as inane.

He claimed to be a member of the *Altor Custodis* and Dante was inclined to believe him on that one score. How else could he have the very specialized information about those events so long ago? Only the society of guardians was known to keep records of such occurrences. Dante supposed there might be a few of his kind still around who might know the circumstances of that fiery night back in 1871, but vampires were usually disinclined to deal with magic users of any sort. Dante thought he would be able to detect the traces of another vampire on the mage, if such were the case. He detected no such taint.

Touching down in Billings, Montana an hour before midnight, Dante arranged for storage of his new custom Lear 60XR jet. It was a honey of an aircraft, built for comfort and speed, and he truly enjoyed taking it out for a spin every now and again. He was a man who appreciated speed.

The vintage Harley that rolled out of the cargo area of his jet a few moments later lent credence to that fact. Dante figured he had about six hours before dawn to meet up with Vabian, scout around his safe house—something he would never trust a human to arrange—and feed before the sun forced him inside. He had a few hours to travel up into the woods on the motorcycle, which he was looking forward to. The empty roads out here invited him to push the bike to its limits and for the first time in years, he felt rumbles of anticipation. It was a clear, star-filled, glorious night with open roads and a powerful machine to help him fly across the ground.

Vabian heard the powerful thrum of the motorcycle as it pulled into the lot across from the small motel where he'd holed up for the duration of this operation. They were just outside the national park in lower Montana. It was cold at night, but bearable. Of course the cold wouldn't matter to Dante, undead creature that he was.

He didn't like the vampire, but he was a means to an end. Without Dante's superior strength and skills, Vabian wouldn't stand much of a chance against the *were*, and he had to get through the *were* to get to the priestess.

He hadn't told Dante his ultimate goal, but his mission was clear. The new priestess had to die. Lilias' legacy could not be allowed to live on in her daughter. Vabian's masters had given him the task of eliminating the girl who had eluded them for so long. It was the first time he'd been entrusted such a momentous task and he would not fail. He'd been working toward this, waiting for his opportunity to climb higher in the ranks of the *Venifucus*. This was his chance to prove himself and he would not—could not—fail.

Oh, he pretended to be a member of the weaker society, the *Altor Custodis*, but they only watched and recorded, never intervening when they knew all too well the monsters whose secrets they guarded. Vabian had started with them and still kept in touch with his contacts there, but as a magic user, he was privy to secrets lesser mortals would never know. He was now part of the *Venifucus*, the magic users blessed with the power and wisdom to reign over all other beings.

They worked in secret for now, but their day was coming. The day when all other beings would bow down before the *Venifucus Priori* and swear allegiance to them alone. On that day, Vabian vowed, he would be one of that exalted number. He would be *A Priori*, elevated over mortals and other magic users to the highest ranks of the *Venifucus*. Only the *Mater Priori* would be greater than he, and she, it was said, was an ancient being of enormous power. He looked forward to her return to this mortal realm. He knew he could distinguish himself with the *Mater Priori*. There were few women who could resist Patrick Vabian, after all, and as her consort, he would have power the likes of which had been unknown in this realm for centuries.

The only thing standing in the way of such glory was the Lady and Her priestesses. And of course, their protectors. It was a goal of all *Venifucus* to kill priestesses wherever they were found and destroy those who would harbor and protect them.

The *Venifucus* had managed to kill off Lilias—the most powerful priestess in millennia because of her twin *were* mates—but their whelp had escaped. Still, much strength had been granted to the *Venifucus* cause by such a glorious triumph. It was rumored the *Paeter Priori* himself had been the one to kill Lilias and her mates. Vabian knew such grand service to the *Venifucus* gained the old man his position of power over all other *Priori*, leading the council and steering the society's course while they plotted for the return of the *Mater*.

Vabian wanted that glory for himself. If he could destroy Lilias' daughter and her newfound mates, it would go a long way toward securing his position. And Vabian would do whatever he needed to in order to achieve his goal—even team with a perverted bloodletter. Once Dante had served his purpose, Vabian would vanquish the vampire as well. He looked forward to the day with relish, even as he opened the door of his cheap hotel suite to invite the ancient one inside.

"Glad you made it."

"I bet." Dante's sarcasm rolled through the small suite as he unzipped his leather jacket. Vabian decided to let the comment pass. Dante's time was coming soon enough.

"Everything's set."

Vabian closed the door and nodded toward a map he had laid out on the room's only table. Dante sauntered over and studied it as Vabian deliberately went to the small refrigerator and pulled out a container of orange juice he'd bought earlier. He knew simple OJ was like acid to the undead but Dante didn't give him the satisfaction of a reaction as Vabian downed half the container with noisy swallows.

"They're in the national park?" Dante looked back at the map.

"On the edge. They have a collection of houses up there. The one we're interested in is highlighted in pink, right there." Vabian leaned over to point one pink highlighter-stained finger at the map he'd been working on for the past hour. "As you can see, there's only one viable approach."

"Maybe for you."

Dante's narrowed eyes held secrets Vabian didn't like. All his information said Dante was a simple vampire with no advanced skills except those he'd had when he turned. He'd been a warrior, a knight, in the twelfth century and was known as a fearless fighter. That's all Vabian needed him for—to keep the *were*wolves occupied in battle while he went after the woman.

"I'd planned to go up through here," Vabian pointed to a route he'd also highlighted in pink, "then cut through the woods a bit to this point so they won't see us coming."

Dante nodded. "Yes. You should take that route." He traced to a point on the map, very near the target house. "I will meet you here. We go together from there."

"But—"

Dante let the map drop back to the table. "I'll meet you there. That's all you need to know." He stepped forward and without conscious thought, Vabian retreated. The vampire smiled in his sinister way. "Now for my payment."

"You just fed from me three days ago. Every five days was our agreement!"

"I'm altering the agreement." Dante stalked him in the small room. "Pray I don't alter it any further."

CREO

Early the next evening, just after sunset, Dante made his way over the trees in the form of a large black hawk. Few, if any, knew he had mastered his powers to the point he could transform into just about any animal he wished, and he wanted to keep the knowledge secret. Those busybody *Altor Custodis*—the Guardians, as some of them called themselves—didn't need to know the full extent of his abilities.

It was his own private triumph that he could float on the air currents as a bird, or even as mist, given an urgent enough reason to tax his strength to such an extent. It wasn't easy to form mist, keep it together and yet separate enough to appear normal. Unless there was some serious threat, Dante preferred to take the more corporeal forms of animals.

Perching high in a large tree, Dante scoped out the target home with his keen hawk's vision. He could sense *were* all around, but saw none. He wondered idly if they realized he was about. Certainly there would have been more activity around the house had the alarm been raised. So far, he was probably undetected, which suited his plans well.

He had an hour or so before he would meet that bumbling human, Vabian. Dante intended to use the time well. He would reconnoiter the home and surroundings, confirming Vabian's information for himself before launching the planned attack.

So far, everything looked just as Vabian had said. Falling out of the tree and transforming into a fluffy grey squirrel on the way to the ground, Dante sniffed the trails around the house, walking right up to the foundation and climbing up the trellis.

Two men and a female inhabited the building. He could scent two *were*wolves, very similar yet just slightly individual. These must be the twins Vabian said were the lords of the *were* for this generation. Dante looked forward to the challenge of fighting them. It'd been too long since he tested his skills against a worthy opponent. Hopefully these two would give him a run for his money.

The female was harder to place. Her scent tasted of *were*, but also of something else. Not wolf, though that made little sense if she were one of the males' mates. Her scent was more complex. *Were*cat perhaps, but then again, perhaps not. There was something strange about her scent that bothered Dante on some basic level.

But his explorations would have to wait. It was almost time to meet up with Vabian, and though Dante didn't care much for the human mage, he was looking forward to the battle ahead. Scurrying away through the undergrowth, Dante waited until he was farther away before shifting shape yet again.

Moments later, he arrived in his human form at the prearranged meeting place. Vabian was already there, pacing.

"Where the hell have you been?"

Dante looked down at the weaker man with disdain.

"The house is unprotected. Only three are within."

"Three? Two men and a woman?"

Dante nodded slowly. Vabian had a fanatical light in his eyes that was mildly disturbing, but then he was one of those self-proclaimed Guardians. Who knew what drove such people?

"Let's go."

Vabian took off through the woods, making more noise than a herd of elephants, but Dante only shrugged and followed. There was little hope a human—even a mage—could approach a house full of *were* without them knowing. Of course a vampire of Dante's age and skill could probably do it, but it wouldn't be easy.

But Dante didn't mind the noise or the warning it would give his prey. He was here for a fight and though he was many things, he wasn't a dishonorable man. When he fought, he fought fair. Or at least, as fair as a centuries-old vampire of superior skill could against youngsters like the *were*wolves he would face tonight.

"Someone's coming." Rafe's head perked up as he stood near the kitchen window, open to let in the early evening breeze. He sniffed the air currents, his hearing picking up sounds only a skilled *were*wolf could hear.

"Not one of ours." Tim nodded, his lips thinning to a tight line as he stood beside his twin.

"Lost hiker?"

Tim shook his head. "Nah, they're trying to sneak up on us. Hikers don't sneak and only humans sneak around so loudly."

Rafe and Tim stalked through the house, pausing at the foot of the stairs. Allie was just coming down but stopped short when they blocked her path, their faces grim.

"What is it?"

"We're not sure yet." Rafe touched her shoulder, wishing he could comfort her, but the tension rode thick in the air. "Could be nothing, but we need you to stay inside. Lock all the doors and windows and if something goes wrong, call Betina on your cell phone. Tell her to mobilize the pack. Then run for Otto's. Take the wooded path. He'll know what to do."

She clutched at his arm. "Are we in danger?"

Tim stepped to her other side. "We don't know yet, but we have to be prepared for anything."

Rafe stroked her hair, taking just a moment to kiss her brow. "There's someone approaching through the woods from the north. They're human and trying to move with stealth, which doesn't bode well for their intentions. We're going out to meet them, but you need to stay here, sweetheart. We need to know where you'll be."

"I don't like this."

Rafe had to smile at her show of backbone. Their mate was feisty, as it should be. He leaned down to give her a quick, smacking kiss.

"Just do it, Allie. For me."

"And for me."

Tim's gruff voice sounded as Allie was yanked gently from Rafe's arms. Rafe grinned as his tough-as-nails brother laid a kiss on Allie that was so hot it could melt iron. He did it fast though, knowing they had to get outside before the approaching threat could get too much closer to their home—and to Allie.

Her expression was dazed as Tim let her go and headed for the door.

"Stay inside," Rafe said with a grin as he followed his twin. He locked the door on his way out for good measure.

Tim signaled to Rafe as they maneuvered around the clumsy human a few moments later. They were closer to the house than they'd like, but it couldn't be helped. The man was forty-ish with straggly blonde hair and a weak chin. He didn't look like much of a threat but the twins took nothing for granted.

The man was clearly trying to tread quietly through the forest, but few humans could pass *were* hearing. Only certain highly skilled woodsmen, a few dedicated magic users and some of the more supernatural inhabitants of the globe even had a chance.

As the thought crossed Tim's mind, so too did the sudden whiff of something...not quite right...reach his sensitive nostrils. He started with alarm as the faint scent of old blood reached him again.

Vampire!

The thought screamed through his brain. This was no simple lost hiker or anything remotely innocent. This was an attack!

"Stop right there." Tim's low, commanding voice halted the human in his tracks as Tim stepped out from behind a tree, directly into his path.

"Oh, you frightened me." The human seemed to want to dissemble.

Tim tipped his head, considering. Could the human be the hunted and not the hunter? Perhaps the bloodletter was after this man and that's why he was stalking through their woods. Or maybe the human was somehow in league with the vampire, though Tim had no idea how that could work. Last he heard, vampires didn't mix well with anyone—particularly not *were,* and humans were only a little better.

"You're on private property."

Tim felt Rafe circling around behind the man. The quick glimpse he had of his twin's eyes told him Rafe too had scented the bloodletter and was staying hidden for now. Rafe would shift, to be ready if needed. They'd run this game many times while hunting. It was familiar to them.

"I didn't mean to trespass."

"Is that so?" Tim appeared at ease, but every muscle in his body was poised to spring.

"If you'll just point me back toward the road, I'll be going." The human turned around in a grand gesture, as if searching for the road that was nowhere nearby. Tim saw the glint of gunmetal against the stranger's dark coat a split second before the shot rang out.

It was enough. That quick glance and his *were* reflexes had him springing out of the way just as a gleaming silver bullet imbedded itself in the tree behind where Tim had been standing.

"Now that's not very nice."

Tim had the satisfaction of seeing the human tackled from behind by Rafe, in wolf form, just seconds later. The man sprawled on the forest floor and Tim snatched up his gun. Emptying the barrel, five more silver bullets trickled down to litter the ground.

"Silver? What do you think we are?"

"*Were*wolves," the human spat as Rafe's claws dug into him. The man couldn't move with over two hundred pounds of angry *were*wolf on his back.

"Now why bother with a puny human when you could fight a much more worthy opponent?"

The new voice came from directly behind Tim.

The trace scent of old blood floated to the *were* twins as Tim spun to face the newcomer.

"We have no quarrel with you, bloodletter."

Tim's voice was firm, as was his stance. He realized this vampire was an old one, from the way he held himself and his ability to move undetected by his sharp *were* senses. There was also a lost quality to his icy eyes that boded ill.

"What if I have a quarrel with you?"

The vampire moved closer, his stride slow and easy, his gestures nonchalant, but Tim knew it was all a ruse. The creature was poised to strike given the least provocation.

"Now what could you possibly have against me? I've never even seen you before."

The vampire shrugged. "It's not you personally, but your kind. You see, many years ago your people killed a very dear friend of mine. I've been waiting for an opportunity to pay the *were* back."

"What has this human got to do with it?" Tim nodded toward where Rafe still had the human pinned, but never took his eyes off the bloodletter.

"He's simply a means to an end. He knew you two were the current lords of the *were*. He agreed to lead me to you so I could leave the *were* leaderless as they left me friendless."

Tim turned that over in his mind. How in the world had this human come by such knowledge? All *were* guarded the alpha primes' identities. It was a sacred trust. But somehow the human had known who they were and where they lived, and he'd teamed with a vampire to get them out of the way.

That could mean only one thing.

"*Venifucus!*"

Tim spat the word, turning to the human with rage, but the vampire chose that moment to spring. It was all Tim could do to dodge the worst of the vampire's blows, panting as he grappled with the immense strength of the ancient creature.

He heard Rafe's howl and saw only a flash of a blade as the human scurried off. The vampire inhaled with a sinister smile as Tim scented his twin's blood and singed fur. A quick glance told him Rafe was stumbling after the man, slowly making his way back toward the house. Someone had to protect Allie!

But Rafe was hurt badly and the vampire was a more than worthy opponent. Whether Rafe would make it in time to protect their mate was doubtful. A pain gripped his heart as he realized his twin could very well be breathing his last at this very moment.

If Rafe failed, it would be up to Tim to fulfill their pledge. Allie's life was on the line, but this damned bloodletter was standing in his way.

With a snarl, Tim renewed the fight. He shifted half-way, gaining strength and deadly claws while remaining on two feet to face his opponent. It wasn't easy to hold this form, but Tim would do anything to save Allie.

Moments later a wicked slash appeared across the vampire's chest. Mild surprise showed on his face for a moment. Nodding, he smiled wickedly.

"First blood is yours, my friend, but I will have the rest. Every last drop."

Dante licked his lips as he advanced. This *were*wolf was good, but he was better. He'd had centuries to develop and perfect his skills, plus vampires were naturally faster than even *were*.

"You can try, bloodsucker, but you won't succeed."

"You have spirit, pup. It's almost a shame to kill you, but I've had a grievance with your kind for over a century. It's time for a little payback."

"You bastard! What grievance do you have against our mate? That's who the human is after. Damned *Venifucus!*" The enraged *were*wolf spat blood from his injured jaw to the ground at Dante's feet in clear challenge. "And you're working with him! He's trying to kill the future High Priestess of the Lady. If your soul isn't damned already, it will be if your cohort succeeds."

Dante stood back, weighing the *were*wolf's shocking words. He knew of the dark deeds of the *Venifucus*. He'd had a nearly disastrous run-in with them three centuries ago, but hadn't heard anything of their doings in decades. He'd thought they were extinct like so many of the other dark societies that had sprung up over the years.

"Who is the High Priestess?" Dante asked cautiously.

The angry *were* stood back, panting. "Betina. But our mate is her successor. She's only just been consecrated. She has few skills as yet."

Dante was rocked to the depths of his damned soul. "Vabian is not merely human. He's a powerful warlock."

"Fuck!" the *were*wolf cursed.

"I didn't know." Dante's anger was slow to burn, but it was heating mightily at the thought that Vabian had used him. "I would never harm a priestess." The stark truth of his words cut through the stillness of the forest as if the very trees held their breath to see what would happen next.

"But you've helped a killer to her door." The *were*wolf advanced on him, coming right up into his face. "The question is, what are you going to do about it now?"

Dante held the *were*wolf's gaze for a long, testing moment, then stepped back.

"Go to your mate. I'll not interfere further."

The *were*wolf nodded, shedding the rest of his clothes. "We'll settle this rest of this later. If she dies, there's no cave deep enough where you can hide from my people."

In a flash, the *were* shifted all the way to the form of a huge wolf and bounded through the trees. Dante watched after him as he disappeared into the forest, cursing the human who had so easily played him.

Dante didn't like being played. He hadn't been so gullible since he'd first been turned and even then, the few who had crossed him had paid with their lives. Eventually.

He wasn't so patient now. The mage would die at his hands, if the *were*wolves didn't get him first. Of course, if the young priestess was already dead, Dante knew his end would soon follow. One didn't aid in the murder of a priestess—even a young one—without consequences.

The end of his existence didn't bother Dante as much as the thought that any small chance at redemption would be forever lost if the girl were killed. Until that moment he hadn't quite realized how much he still craved that ultimate reward, the return to the ranks of the blessed rather than the damned. Suddenly he wanted that chance more than anything and he saw it slipping through his hands. If the girl died, so too would his chance.

Her mates were strong fighters, but Dante couldn't trust his own fate to them. One was already badly wounded and the other might not have the skill to face a magic user of Vabian's caliber.

There was only one thing to do.

Dante harnessed his power and shifted. A sleek, midnight black wolf sped through the forest a moment later, fast on the heels of the *were*wolf.

Chapter Eight

Something was wrong. Allie heard the pitiful yelping as Rafe, in wolf form, staggered onto the porch. He was bleeding badly and growling at her in a way that told her to stay inside even as she came to the door.

Only seconds later, a huge fireball hit the side of the porch, just missing Rafe. Sparks rained down to dissipate harmlessly against the wood, though the whole house shook with the force of the blow.

Magic!

Allie felt a tingling in her newly awakened senses. This was not good. The flavor of this magic, the scent of it, turned her stomach. She was confronting evil. Allie looked up to see a man approaching from the woods, a flashing silver blade in his hands, dripping with what she could only assume was Rafe's blood. But where was Tim?

The man raised his arm and she saw the bright ball of orange flame form in the palm of his hand just before he lobbed it at the house. Again the solid structure rocked on its frame, and Rafe growled deep in his throat, placing himself squarely between the danger and Allie.

But he was wounded! Allie saw the blood flowing out of him and the dark stain of the wound that would have crippled any normal creature. The magic user raised his arm once more and

Allie's heart lumped in her throat as she saw the man aim for Rafe as he slunk down the steps to open ground, in a brave, last-ditch effort to stop the man.

In a moment of foolish courage, Allie stepped from the comparative safety of the house and ran down the porch steps. She jumped at Rafe a split second before the man let loose with a huge ball of magical energy—glad when he redirected it to her instead of poor, injured Rafe. Allie poured all her energy into the shield she'd been learning to construct as her feet hit the ground.

She thought it was all over for her, but to her amazement, the rudimentary shield held. She looked up to see the sparks dissipating in a sphere around where she stood. The mage stopped dead in his tracks.

"What do you want?" Allie faced the man with all the courage she could muster, though she was shaking on the inside.

"I want you dead."

The strange mage launched another volley directly at her but the firebolts bounced off the circular shield that formed like a bubble around her body. Even as she ducked, the bolts came nowhere near her, repulsed about a foot away. She felt the power though, draining her own newly discovered energy and she knew she couldn't take many more hits like this.

She had to get to Rafe. He was trying to stand and fight, but he was far too weak. Allie prayed like never before, using the words Betina had taught her as she called upon the Lady she served for the first time in dire need.

Raising one hand, she felt the power gathering and flowing through her, pulsing out in a wave that knocked the mage to his knees, his expression stricken. At the same time, Rafe stood, renewed by the energy wave, not completely well, but better than he'd been.

"Come to me, my love." Allie's whispered words drew Rafe to her, within the circle of her protection. She clutched him close as he collapsed in front of her, panting heavily. He faced the mage, baring his teeth and snarling as the man tried to rise once more to his feet. Allie clutched Rafe by the fur of his neck in fear.

"Stay with me, Rafael," she whispered as she bent only slightly to reach his ear. "Tim is coming. Stay with me, my love. We'll protect each other."

Tim broke through the line of trees in time to see the mage regain his feet. A quick glance showed him Allie was right in the line of fire. His heart raced and caught in his throat to see her outside the safety of the house. But Rafe was with her, guarding her, though he looked to be in bad shape.

Howling mightily, Tim launched himself at the mage's back, dropping him face first onto the ground, but Tim's momentum took him a few feet past the man. Tim spun but the mage was already up, his hands outstretched as he muttered his curses, aiming his dark energies at Tim.

Good. That's just what he wanted. He'd gladly trade his life to give Rafe a chance to get Allie to safety. She was the most important thing here. Her safety meant all. Plus, human magic wasn't quite as effective against *were* as it would be against Allie. This warlock would have to be powerful indeed to be able to take down an alpha *were*wolf with his magic alone.

But he still had that silver blade. Tim saw it almost too late as he swerved to avoid the same poisonous blow that had nearly done in his brother. Landing awkwardly, Tim had a hard time regaining his feet. The slight hesitation could have cost him his life, but the mage was otherwise occupied.

Tim heard a crashing roar and then a huge black wolf was on the mage, tearing for his throat. The wolf didn't smell quite right to Tim's *were* senses, but a moment later he realized why as the vampire shifted form, pinning the human beneath him.

"Do you want to die slow or fast?" the vampire asked the struggling man.

To give Vabian credit, the mage mustered his strength and continued to fight until the bloodletter snapped his arm like a normal person would snap a dry twig. He stilled after that and the vampire let up a bit.

"Slow or fast, human? You've crossed me and I intend to have justice."

The vampire's cold voice sent shivers down even Tim's spine.

"How about not at all?" Tim saw only a flash as the mage raised the bloody silver knife in his other hand, slashing down on the vampire with surprising strength.

The bloodletter jerked and let go of the mage, rising to his feet as the silver blade caused a sharp, deadly reaction in his ancient body. Silver was poisonous to *were* and vampire alike, it seemed.

The mage scrambled away and Tim was torn. He wanted to go after the mage and kill him for what he'd done to his brother and end the threat to Allie, but he couldn't leave Allie unprotected with Rafe so badly hurt and a strange, wounded bloodletter nearby. Who knew what the vampire was capable of?

Making his decision and marking the trail well in his mind, Tim let the human go, looking to the wounded vampire as he leaned heavily against a tree, breathing harshly. Tim allowed the change to come over him until he faced the vampire in human form.

"The mage will die."

Tim nodded. "If not today, then as soon as possible."

"See to your woman." The vampire jerked his chin in Allie's direction. "Your brother does not look well."

As alpha, Tim didn't take orders well—or at all, really—but he saw the sense in the ancient one's words. Moving to where Rafe lay quietly panting and obviously in serious pain, Tim brushed himself off and helped Rafe and Allie into the house. He picked up the phone and dialed for help immediately. He called on the pack to protect Betina and request she come to help treat Rafe's wounds.

He spared a few seconds to put on a pair of jeans and headed back outside. The vampire was still out there and had to be dealt with. Without his help, things could have turned out much worse. Yet he'd been instrumental in getting the magic user close enough to launch his attack. It was a sticky situation, to be sure.

Ambling down the porch steps, Tim found the vampire on the edge of the clearing that was the front yard of the house. He was still leaning against that same tree, apparently trying to gather his strength.

"Thanks for your intervention." Tim nodded, keeping a wary distance.

"It's the least I could do." The ghost of a smirk passed the vampire's lips.

"I'm Tim and that was my brother, Rafe. We are indebted to you for helping save the life of our mate. Her name is Allie."

"Forgive me," the vampire whispered, clearly shaken and gravely injured. "I didn't know what Vabian was up to or I would never have come."

"What can you tell us about him?" Tim's voice was hard in the eerily silent forest.

"His name is Patrick Vabian. He claimed to be *Altor Custodis* when he came to see me several weeks ago. He knew enough of my past to make me believe him and he offered me the one thing he knew would tempt me."

"Us?"

The bloodletter nodded. "Your predecessors killed someone very dear to me. I've wanted justice for a very long time."

"I'm sorry for your loss but you have to understand, Rafe and I had nothing to do with it. We didn't kill your friend. We never even knew him. But I promise you this—whatever our predecessors may have done to wrong you, we will try to make amends if your cause is just and it's within our power. We owe you that much."

The vampire nodded, gritting his teeth in pain and losing strength rapidly. "I am Dante d'Angleterre. The death for which I seek justice is that of a firewitch named Erik Watson on October 8, 1871."

"You seem to associate with a lot of magic users."

"I do not make a habit of it, I assure you, but Erik was as a brother to me. He was the reincarnation of the brother I lost centuries ago. His death—" The vampire broke off, clearly choked by emotion, and perhaps more than his share of pain. He swallowed hard before continuing in a stronger voice. "It wounded me greatly."

Tim nodded. "We'll look into it. There are some chronicles from that time we can access, given a few days."

The vampire looked as drained as any being Tim had ever seen. He was literally white as snow as his blood drained away through the seeping wounds in his side that he clutched with both hands.

"Will you be okay?"

"I know a safe place not far."

"But don't you need blood?"

Just the word made the vampire's eyes glow and his nostrils flare.

"Are you offering?"

Tim considered the bloodletter carefully. "I've heard that *were* blood is more potent to your kind than others, and I do owe you. I can't give you much, but I'm willing if it will help you get to your safehouse."

"Then I gladly accept. You should know though, this will bond us, just slightly."

"You helped protect my mate. There are few deeper bonds than that for a *were*wolf." Tim stepped up and offered his left wrist to the pale vampire. "Do what you need to do."

Tim braced himself but when Dante bit down there was only one sharp jolt of pain, quickly replaced with a warm sizzle that felt almost pleasant. He watched the bloodletter's mouth work as he sucked in the life giving fluid, and was amazed by the quick return of color to the snow white skin.

Dante stopped feeding much sooner than Tim expected and he knew this ancient being was a man of deeply rooted honor. The clues were all there, from the way Dante had let Vabian's stumbling in the forest alert the brothers to their approach, to the way he took only what he needed so Tim wouldn't be left too weak to protect his family.

"You have my thanks, *Were*Lord."

"Call me Tim."

The vampire bowed respectfully, though his haunting eyes stayed focused on Tim. He rubbed at his wrist, amazed to see no trace of the twin incisions that had been there only moments before. Even he didn't normally heal this fast.

"We will meet again. I owe your lady and your brother an apology."

Tim nodded. "And we all owe Patrick Vabian some retribution."

"Too true."

"Do you have transportation?"

Dante sighed. "I flew here."

"Well, I'll be damned. You can shift into more than just a wolf?"

"That is a secret I hope you will keep close. Few, if any, know of my full abilities. Vabian didn't know I could shift, though he had intimate details about my past. Hopefully my secret will die with him. Soon."

Tim threw him a set of keys from his pocket. "Take my bike. It's in the back shed and small enough that you can take it indoors so no one will know where you're holed up. I'd have offered my truck, but I figured you'd refuse."

A rare smile crossed the vampire's face. "You're a clever man. Thanks for the loan."

Five minutes later, Dante was gone and the first of the pack began to arrive with reinforcements. Tim deputized Rocky to sort out patrols while he went back inside to his badly wounded brother and mate. Betina was on her way, he knew. They would need her skill and strength to even begin healing Rafe. Tim had taken a quick look at his brother's wounds and knew they were well beyond his ability to patch up. Plus, magic wounds usually defied the *were*'s natural ability to heal. Such wounds called for a specialist—a mage healer or a priestess of the Lady.

Betina arrived just a short while later, heavily guarded by more than her usual compliment of *were*. Tim was glad to see his people were taking no chances with the chosen of the Lady, even without an explicit order. They all knew how precious these special women were to their kind, and the greater world. That Betina chose to live so close with his people was a blessing they never took for granted.

"Who did this?" Betina was all business as she checked Rafe's wounds. Allie had already begun to clean him off, but her tears were a constant thing.

Tim pulled Allie into his arms, holding her back against his front as they watched Betina work on Rafe, now blessedly unconscious. His fur was burned away in places, matted with blood in others, and a huge gash wound down his belly, bleeding freely.

"A warlock named Patrick Vabian."

Betina worked briskly, examining Rafe carefully before proceeding.

"This was made with a silver blade."

Tim's arms tightened around Allie reflexively.

"Will he live?" Tim asked.

"It'll be a close thing." Betina's old eyes sought his and fear for his twin escalated. "Allesandra, my dear, come to me."

Betina's hand reached out and Tim reluctantly let her go. Allie's tears still tracked down her face, but her breathing eased a bit as Betina gave her something to focus on other than her sorrow. Tim knew Allie was scared. Hell, he was scared too, but Betty was the High Priestess. If anyone could save his twin, she could.

Allie felt fear like she'd never known. Rafe, so brave, so strong, so loving, lay dying. She could actually feel his life slipping away. She turned tearful eyes to Betina as the older woman took her hand.

"We have to save him."

"I know, dear." Betina patted her hand and led her to stand on one side of the bed while she moved to stand across from her on Rafe's other side. "Tim, stand at the foot of the bed to ground him here in this realm with you."

Betina took one of Rafe's big front paws in her hand and motioned Allie to do the same on the other side, then she reached out to complete the circle, clasping Allie's free hand in hers. Allie felt the jolt of connection as the circle was closed and the energy pulsed slowly between all three of them.

Betina began to chant softly. Allie followed her in the words she had learned so recently. A hauntingly beautiful song, Allie knew it was designed to call upon the magic of the earth and the forest as well as that of the spirit realms. She felt the power build slowly, felt the increase in the pulsations between her and Betina—and Rafe.

The power built and built and Allie watched in awe as a subtle glow of sparkling golden energy surrounded Betina, revealing her inner nature to Allie's newly trained second sight. She saw the faint outline of gossamer wings folded serenely at the woman's side.

Betina was fey!

Betina's wise eyes moved to Allie's and she nodded once, acknowledging her student's discovery with a gentle smile. Allie felt the renewed surge of the energies Betina and she called, then marveled as the older woman shaped them and redirected them away from the two women and into Rafe. Allie felt herself opening like a conduit, her spirit guiding the healing energies to her mate with all the love and care in her being.

She looked down at Rafe, seeing with new eyes the angry red of the slash across his abdomen. It oozed black energy, sapping his strength, spreading like a stain over his soul. It looked like evil, if such a thing had form, and it broke her heart to see her lover so gravely wounded.

The golden glow increased, sparks of dazzling energy pinging off the three of them, but when they reached out toward Tim, standing tall and silent at the foot of the bed, they were redirected back to the trio. Tim was grounding them, containing their energy by his steadfast presence, Allie realized. He was their link to the mortal realm and their protector. He stood over all of them while they tarried in magics not of this realm, containing and protecting with his strength of spirit, his honorable soul and his boundless love for both his brother and his mate.

Betina wound down the chant, pulling back from the tenuous connections with the spirit realms. Allie felt drained, but good about what they had done. Rafe had more color and the angry red of the slashing wound was starting to subside. The black stain was gone, banished by the sparkling golden energy that surrounded him still.

Slowly, his eyes blinked open, his long tongue licking out around canine teeth. Allie collapsed to her knees at the side of his bed, her hands stroking over his soft fur.

"Oh, Rafe!"

She felt the shift in energies as Rafe changed to his human form and knew he wouldn't have had the power to do it without Betina's infusion of otherworldly energy. Rafe was bloody, bruised, but no longer in mortal peril. His tanned skin was pale, his eyes sunken, but his smile was genuine, if weak.

"Don't cry, sweetheart." His hand stroked softly over her cheek.

Tim snapped a blanket over his brother, tucking it around his feet and up to his waist.

"Glad to see you awake, brother."

Tim's voice was gruff, his eyes suspiciously moist as he came up behind Allie and knelt, folding her in his arms as he reached around to grasp his brother's hand. Allie turned her face up to his and kissed one stubbly cheek. Tim was such a tough guy, but inside, he was a deep and caring man. He was closer to his twin than anyone on earth and she loved them both dearly.

She turned back and leaned down to kiss Rafe as well.

"How do you feel?"

"Like I got run over by a truck." He moved one hand to scratch at his chest, looking down in surprise when his hand came away wet with blood. "Holy shit. What happened?"

"How much do you remember?" Betina asked quietly, still at the other side of the bed.

Rafe's eyes clouded in thought, then widened in alarm. "That human! And the vampire! Did you kill them?"

"Vampire?" Betina was clearly shocked by the revelation.

Tim's arms tightened around Allie before he spoke.

"The bloodletter is no threat to us. His name is Dante. The mage was using him to keep us occupied while he went after Allie. Dante even helped me save her, though it wounded him badly. The mage was injured, but ran when faced with Dante and me fighting together against him."

"You said the mage's name was Vabian?" Betina asked quietly.

Tim nodded and Allie felt the motion against her hair, comforting even as they discussed such serious matters. How she loved this strong, difficult man!

"Dante and I talked just before the cavalry arrived. He told me the man's name and how he came to be here. He also apologized. He had no idea Vabian was using him and he was royally pissed. I'd say Vabian's days are numbered with both the *were* and a pissed off vampire after him." Tim's voice was pitched low and deadly near Allie's ear though all in the room heard him.

"He can't die too soon for me." Rafe's eyes had a hardness Allie had never seen in them. In that moment she saw the same deadly determination in the more carefree twin's eyes that she was used to seeing in his brother's.

"*Venifucus* slime," Tim cursed.

"*Venifucus*? What's that mean?" Grim faces met Allie's question.

Betina sighed heavily. "They are an ancient society. They are the main threat to our existence. The *Venifucus* are dedicated to what I would call pure evil. They want power above all and we, as priestesses of the Lady, stand in their way."

"It was their agents who murdered your mother and her mates," Tim said quietly.

"They're part of the reason I never go anywhere alone, Allesandra." Betina's voice was soft, as if she hated what she had to say. "They've tried to kill me more than a few times over the years."

"So you've always had bodyguards?"

"Me?" Betina laughed. "Heavens no. In the old days I could stand up to just about anything and I was quicker than anything they sent after me. Only during my training did I require help, as you do now, and as I get older and not quite so

140

quick-footed, I find it comforting to have friends available should I need help. I'm not as spry as I used to be."

Rafe reached out a hand to the older woman. "You're just as powerful as ever, Lady Betina, and you always will be."

Allie realized Rafe's kind words were probably more accurate than he knew. If she could believe what she'd seen, Betina was fey, and therefore, probably immortal.

CRSO

A short while later, Allie helped Rafe clean up a bit more and settled him into a nice, freshly made bed for recuperative sleep. Still very weak, he had a lot of serious bruises and cuts to heal, though he was out of danger for now. Betina said all he needed now was rest and the *were*'s natural healing abilities would have him good as new within a few days.

When Allie went back into the living room to see what Tim was up to, she found a war council of sorts already in session. The alphas from each of the local tribes and clans were present, including her uncles, gathered around Tim and Betina, planning strategies to track and take out Patrick Vabian.

Her Uncle Tom spotted her in the doorway and came over to tug her into a fierce hug.

"I'm so glad you're all right," he whispered into her ear as he hugged her.

She could tell from the tightness of his arms and the slight trembling in his voice he was probably remembering how he'd lost his brothers and sister-in-law to a similar attack.

"I'm all right, *Tio*," Allie kissed Tom's cheek as he let her go, only to be patted on the back by Ryan, her aunt Jilly's mate. Both men wore serious expressions filled with relief as she smiled up at them, squeezing their hands in reassurance.

After a moment more with them, Allie quietly took her seat at Tim's side, glad when he pulled her close against him with one strong arm around her waist. He bent down and absently kissed the top of her head even as he listened to what one of the alpha *were*cats was saying. They were discussing the vampire, she realized, and Tim's tensions were rising. She could feel it in the arm tightening just slightly around her waist.

"How do we know he didn't come here to prey on our kind?" the *were*cat's voice rang with anger and suspicion. "I've heard stories about how bloodletters get high from *were* blood. I don't want to see any of my clan victimized by a rogue vampire in our territory."

Tim cleared his throat. "Dante is not to be harmed. I gave him safe passage—and my bike—so if you see him on it, don't worry. He put himself at great risk to save Allie and Rafe. Me too, for that matter. His wounds were terrible." Tim's eyes clouded with memory. "I gave him my blood so he could at least get away." Shocked silence met Tim's bold statement. "It's true. *Were* blood is more potent to his kind than human blood, but he wasn't high. He was barely able to walk upright from the pain of his injuries, and he proved himself a man of honor. He only took what he needed from me so he would be able to get away safely."

"He drank your blood? Could you be under his spell?" Hank, the alpha *were*eagle, was clearly suspicious.

Betina cleared her throat. "Vampires are able to bedazzle their prey, but *were* are not very susceptible to their brand of magic. Alphas least of all. I'd say Tim knew exactly what he was doing and while I'm not fond of bloodletters, I'd have to say all I've heard of this Dante leads me to lend him the benefit of the doubt in this case at least."

"Dante said he came here to seek justice over a death our ancestors sanctioned. A firewitch named Erik that was like a brother to him. He died at *were* hands in October of 1871."

"Those were dark days. Dark days indeed." Betina shook her head.

Allie thought through her history. "That was the month and year of the Great Chicago Fire."

"Indeed," Betina's eyes held terrible memories, "and the fight with Erik was responsible for the fire. The prime alphas of that time—Gillen and Roy—cougars they were, sentenced the young mage to death. They mistakenly thought he was responsible for the rape and murder of one of their clan, but it was later proven to be someone else. If the bloodletter seeks justice for Erik's death, he has just cause. Gillen and Roy killed that boy, and as he tried to defend himself with his one true magic—fire—he started an inferno that burned more than half of Chicago." Betina looked around the room, her gaze steady as she deliberately made eye contact with each alpha present to drive home the seriousness of her words. "Your ancestors made an unforgivable mistake. The world lost an innocent young mage that day, not to mention the human and property losses, and they gravely offended an ancient and powerful bloodletter."

Silence reigned as her words sank in.

"I've seen the man fight." Allie's words poured into the tense room. "He stepped in when he could have just as easily sat back and let us all be killed. I think he realized his mistake and did what he could to rectify it. I'm with Betty. I'll give him the benefit of the doubt." There was some grumbling but quite a few faces held grudging acceptance with two priestesses now speaking out in favor of the vampire. "Our real problem, as I see it, is the *Venifucus*."

Allie's innocent words started a firestorm as the gathered *were* reacted with various forms of alarm and anger.

"*Venifucus!* I thought they were all dead!" Her Uncle Tom's dismay could be heard across the large room

"They are not gone." Betina bowed her head as the room calmed, waiting to hear what she would say. "The mage Vabian is undoubtedly one of their number. Else he couldn't have targeted Allie so astutely."

"He must be found and dealt with," Tim's voice was strong and firm, "but I don't want any of you going solo. This guy took on Rafe and me together and we didn't do too well. If not for Dante's help and Allie shielding Rafe, one or more of us could have died. I don't want to lose any of you, or any of your families, to this bastard." Tim reached forward to the coffee table and unrolled what looked to Allie like a large topographical map of the area. "If we do this, we do it in packs. We track him and tackle him in force, but be wary, he knows what we are and he knows our weaknesses. He slashed Rafe with a silver knife within the first few moments of contact. His gun was loaded with silver bullets. I'm sure he has other tricks up his sleeve to make up for the fact that we're more resistant to his magic than most."

"Resistant, yes, but not bulletproof," Betina warned. "He will use magic against you where and when he can, as diversion if nothing else. Be wary."

Tim scooted forward on the sofa as all the others gathered around the map and they began dividing up territory. They would track Vabian's every step as far as they could, keeping in touch by cell phone and radio, appointing a liaison and a backup within each group, assigning them a particular hunting range.

The military precision with which Tim and his subordinates strategized impressed Allie. They quickly formulated a plan of attack that would make a general proud. Knowing she could contribute little to this phase of the planning, Allie excused herself to go sit with Rafe. She lay down on top of the cover, within touching distance, but far enough away not to disturb her healing mate.

Within moments, she was fast asleep.

Chapter Nine

Allie woke to warmth and the bristly feeling of male whiskers against her bare skin. Being naked was the first thing she noticed. Then she became aware of the soft heat being generated by rough male hands moving over her thighs.

"Mmm, Allie, you're so good to wake up to." Rafe's voice floated gently over her senses, warming her from the inside out.

"How are you feeling?" She leaned up on her elbows to look over his damaged body. His wounds were already fading, only a long pink line showing now where yesterday he'd been cut, bleeding, and near death.

"I'm good, but I'd be even better if you'd bring that pretty pussy over here and sit on my lap."

The fire in his eyes dared her.

"Rafe, you almost died yesterday."

"All the more reason to fuck today."

"Rafe!" She squealed when he lifted her by the waist and settled her astride him. "Stop that. You'll hurt yourself!"

He rubbed his hips—and the long hardness between— against her folds. She couldn't deny the wetness flowing from her at his bold move, but he'd been so near death. It didn't seem possible he was well enough in just one night to be up for the kind of mischief his daring expression warranted.

"Rafe, you've got to take it easy." She pushed at his shoulders and he let her move back a little, but not much. Just far enough so he could push the fingers of one hand into her slit, teasing and tugging on her clit, raising her temperature and her appetites to an almost unbearable height. His other hand teased one nipple, while his mouth moved in to kiss the other with little nibbling bites interspersed with lapping licks.

"Rafael! I'm not kidding around." She tried to grab his head, sinking her fingers into his lush hair, but he was undeterred.

"I need you, Allie," he whispered against her breast, his voice tortured and so deeply masculine she felt herself growing wetter by the moment.

"Rafe, I don't want to hurt you." She was pleading with him now as his fingers invaded her core, sliding through the evidence of her arousal.

He moved back then, looking into her eyes. "The only thing that could hurt me is if you turn away from me. Allie, I need you. I'm a desperate man."

"You're an injured man," she corrected him. "You almost died just yesterday."

"Correction on two points. First, I'm not a man. I'm a *were*wolf. And second, I *was* injured yesterday. Today I'm fine. That's where we *were*wolves have it over regular men. We heal fast and without much scarring." He tugged her hand up to his chest, following the faint line of the knife slash that had nearly killed him. Indeed it was nearly healed. "Come on, Allie, give me some of that sweet pussy. You know you want to."

She laughed at the comical look on his face, leaning down to kiss him even as he shifted, removing his fingers and bringing her core right up against the tip of his hard cock. She gave in and slid down on him as his tongue speared into her mouth. She moaned as she took him fully, seating herself on his cock as her breasts pressed into his hard chest.

Suddenly, Tim was behind her, too close. He was freaking her out. Did he want to—?

"Shh, Allie," Rafe soothed her as he broke the kiss. "It'll be okay. I promise."

"We need to do this now, Allie. I'm sorry. We can't give you any more time." Tim's voice was a rough whisper against her ear. "We need to join with you fully."

She'd known this was coming, but still, it frightened her. These men were as close to her as anyone ever had been, or ever would be. She wanted them in her life for all time and wanted to be all things to them as well. Fear was the only thing holding her back, but it wasn't fear of them. It was more a fear of the unknown.

She breathed deeply, gathering her courage. She had to face this fear and get past it—one way or the other. She knew they would stop if there was any question of hurting her. It all came down to trust, she realized, and she had that for them. That and a deep, abiding love.

"It's okay," she whispered. "I trust you."

Tim sighed heavily as he moved even closer. She felt something cool and wet slide into her anus and then a sense of slippery fullness.

"It's just lubricant, sweetheart. It'll make this easier for you."

She felt Rafe's hands spreading her for his brother as he held her against his chest. His lips sought hers and he kissed her deeply while Tim positioned his hard cock at the entrance that had never been breached by a cock before. She felt the pressure of him, the relentless pressing as he sought entrance.

"Push out, Allie. Take him into you," Rafe whispered against her lips as he nibbled his way over her cheek to her ear.

His sharp teeth scraped against the cords in her neck, shooting her excitement higher as she followed his instructions, and suddenly Tim was in, the head of his cock pushing past the tight ring of muscle. The feeling was amazing. With Rafe inside her pussy and now Tim pushing his way into her virgin ass, she felt indescribably full. It burned, but it was a good burn, an exciting burn that eased into a kind of pleasure she'd never known.

"Almost there, baby."

"Fuck!" Rafe cursed against her throat as Tim pushed all the way home, the brothers separated by only the thin wall of her body.

"That's one word for it."

Her mumble made them all chuckle, even as the men started to move inside her. They picked up a rhythm that had one thrusting while the other retreated, one filling her while the other gave way, one pushing in while the other slid out. She felt her excitement rising higher and higher. It was the most incredible feeling!

She also felt them connecting on a different plane altogether. She was still a novice in her abilities, but after the way she'd been called upon to shield Rafe and herself, and the high-level healing Betty had performed with her help, she was more aware of the ethereal plane than ever before.

Allie felt the twin souls that were Rafe and Tim—joined together as they had always been—now moving to encompass her spirit as well. Their light welcomed her, their power warmed her, their love made her soul their own as theirs joined with hers, never to be separate again. They were three, but now they were truly one.

She was awed by the feeling as their souls moved into alignment, even as their bodies strained together toward some unreachable star. She was with them every step of the way, beyond pain or worry, moving into a realm of pure passion, pure sensation, pure love.

"Now, Allie," Rafe coaxed as her eyes opened. "Come with us now, my love."

"I love you both so much!" she cried as she felt herself being swept up in the wave of desire.

Tim bent down over her back, his teeth going to the other side of her neck as Rafe's returned to bite down, gently at first, then harder as his canine teeth lengthened in a partial shift. Vast and uncontrollable powers guided their actions as the twins shifted only a tiny bit to pierce her tender skin with their teeth, marking her as their own for all to see.

Her blood smeared across their lips as all three of them reached a magnificent, simultaneous orgasm. They were joined now, fully and completely, on every level. They knew each other's needs and desires, even as they knew their own.

The twins came hard inside her welcoming body and Allie reveled in each groan of pleasure, each tremor of her own spasming womb. She cried as she came, shouting her love for them both over and over as they rode her body to the highest point it had ever achieved.

They lay there, replete and utterly exhausted. Tim made the effort to roll them all to their sides so they could recover enough to disengage.

As he laid her gently on her side, his cock slowly deflated inside her, Tim licked her neck, bringing his lips up to her ear.

"I love you, Allie." The whisper sounded as if it were wrenched from the depths of his soul. She wanted to turn and face him, but he stilled her. "I've never said that to a woman before. I've never wanted to say it. But I love you with all my heart, Allie, and I always will." Tim kissed her ear, her cheek, her neck softly as he settled behind her.

She was speechless. She'd felt the love radiating off both men, but Tim was so much more reserved than Rafe. She'd doubted he'd ever find the wherewithal to voice the feelings she hoped lay inside. He'd just given her a gift—a rare and priceless gift.

Allie felt tears tracking over her cheeks and Rafe licked them away with gentle kisses.

"I love you too, Allie. Don't be sad."

"I'm not sad."

"Then why the tears?" Rafe asked.

"She's crying?" Tim leaned over, his beloved face tight with concern. "Dammit, baby, did we hurt you?"

"No," she protested as Tim and Rafe both pulled slowly, as gently as they could, from her cooling body. "No, you didn't hurt me."

Both men stared down at her as she swept the stray tears from her face.

"Then why are you crying? Didn't you like it?" Tim stroked her hair with gentle fingers.

"I loved every minute of it." She took each of their hands in hers. "I love you." She kissed their knuckles in turn, loving the confused expressions on their identical faces. "I'm crying because my heart is overflowing with happiness. I'm overloading on joy." She sat up and the tears flowed even more freely as Rafe supported her on one side, Tim on the other. "I never dreamed I'd have love like this in my life."

"Neither did we," Rafe said softly, stroking her thigh almost absently with one large hand.

"I'd given up on it completely," Tim admitted, shocking her gaze up to his. "But then I met you. Allie." His hand stroked her cheek as his head dipped. "I do love you."

He kissed her then, long and deep, warming her from the inside out. When he released her, he passed her comfortably into Rafe's arms for a similar salute. Rafe's tongue probed and prodded at hers in a sensual, almost lazy way that comforted as well as aroused.

"I love you, baby," Rafe said as he released her.

Tim took over then, tucking her in between them as they all lay back on the big bed, exhausted from the energetic sex and emotional revelations of the morning.

"How are you feeling, Rafe?" Allie worried again, now that the overwhelming arousal had been sated.

"Better than new. Between the healing and our joining, I'm a new *were*wolf entirely." He scratched at his healing chest. "An exhausted *were*wolf, but a happy one. I've got my mate joined to me now and no one will ever part us."

Tim's voice sounded from her other side. "That's what the joining is all about. Now that we've had our teeth in your skin, your blood in our mouths, your essence merging with ours, we can never lose you. You bear our mark and our scent and on a deeper level, we're joined soul to soul. Or so the priestesses say."

"I felt that," she remembered with a bit of awe. "When you bit me, when we all...when we came," she felt her cheeks heat with the memory, "I felt our souls bond. It was so beautiful."

"No more beautiful than you, my Allie," Rafe whispered as he stroked the last of the tears from her cheeks, lying on his side looking at her. As she lay on her back, both brothers flanked her, propped up on their elbows, just watching her.

Tim bent to examine the bite marks on her neck. They were tender, but not painful, surprisingly.

"You're already almost healed." Tim's voice rang with satisfaction. "When we bit you, some of our abilities transferred. Over the next few days, they'll begin to manifest."

"I won't become a *were*wolf, will I?" She was only half joking. All those old movies she'd seen as a kid said the bite of a *were*wolf would turn you into one yourself.

Rafe chuckled. "Only if we're really lucky. But most likely you'll just notice you heal quicker. Maybe your senses will sharpen a bit. You might notice scents more strongly or be able to see farther or in darker surroundings than before. Maybe all of the above."

"Don't you know for sure what to expect?"

Tim sighed. "Not really. Our kind don't mate with humans very often. Each case is different, and being that you're already half-*were* and half mage, we can't really say what will happen."

"But we'll be with you through it all," Rafe promised. "If you find you can suddenly shift, we'll help you through it, even if you do turn into a cat." The disgust in his voice as he said that last word was something he couldn't quite hide and she had to laugh.

The idea of being able to shift both appealed to her and scared her half to death. It was such an awesome thought! But she was mated to *were*wolves. Her ancestry was cougar. If she did gain the ability to shift, would she turn into a big cat? And how would that work if her mates were wolves?

"Don't worry about it now, Allie. It'll all work out," Rafe promised her, dipping to place a kiss on her hair.

"I hope you're right." She lay back and closed her eyes, letting the satiated weariness take her into the land of dreams.

CRICO

The sorcerer Vabian licked his wounds, employing some of his magic to speed the healing of his broken arm. The vampire would pay, he vowed. How dare he turn on Patrick Vabian? Dante d'Angleterre didn't know who he'd messed with, but he would find out.

In the meantime, Vabian did careful reconnaissance. He knew if the young priestess were here, the old one wouldn't be far behind. If he couldn't get to the young one right away, he might yet be able to pull off a coup by killing the hag. Then he would gain the power he so desperately wanted among the *Venifucus*.

Vabian's chance came later that day when he caught the old woman coming out of the local grocery store. She was alone, though she usually had company of one sort or another. This time though, she was blessedly alone for at least a few minutes.

Vabian made his move. Stalking the older woman quietly, using advanced magic to hide his presence, he came right up to her in the crowded parking lot behind the store.

"Stop right there, witch." His voice cut through the silence, stilling the woman's steps as she turned to face him.

Funny, she looked younger than he'd thought she'd be. All the data he could find on her in the *Venifucus* records—which admittedly wasn't much—indicated she'd been active as a priestess for quite a number of years.

"What did you call me?"

"I know what you are. Priestess, witch, it's all the same. And you'll die all the same."

The woman laughed, hurting his ears with her tinkling trill. She made him angry too, with her disrespect, but he would show her.

Calling on his magic, he launched a preliminary fireball at her, just to test her shields. Stronger than he'd expected, his energies rolled off and away from her. Away from him too, as she shrewdly directed the power away from them both, back down into the earth.

"Think you're smart, huh?" Vabian launched his next attack, a piercing stab of energy that he was happy to see, weakened her shields considerably, causing the woman to jump back as his energy burned her just slightly.

"Now you've done it," she said, balling her little fists. She really was a tiny thing, he mused, not much to look at to wield so much power. "I warn you now, boy. Turn around and go home. Leave me and my people alone. The *were* and those who serve the Lady are in no danger from the likes of you. Leave us be and we might be persuaded to let you live."

"You talk tough for an old broad."

"Oh, no need to be insulting. You wouldn't want to make me angry."

"Why not? You priestesses are all bark and no bite."

"I may not bite," she had the audacity to chuckle, "buy my protectors will, when they learn what you've done."

"They're not very good protectors if I managed to get you alone."

The woman sighed dramatically, annoying him. He realized in that moment she was stalling him for some reason—probably hoping those "protectors" of hers would come save her skinny little ass. Patrick Vabian wouldn't fall for that!

"Enough talk, witch. Prepare to die."

She laughed in his face, pissing him off. "Now that's rich. What are you going to do? Talk me to death?"

"No, witch. I have better plans." Pulling the silver blade he'd prepared specially for this task, he pointed it at the witch, satisfaction running through him as he watched her face pale.

This was the blade that had already tasted both *were* and vampire blood. This was the blade that he'd consecrated to the darkness, the *Venifucus* and the *Priori*. This was the blade that could harness and direct enough power to kill even a High Priestess.

He called his dark energies to him, funneling them into the blade and outward to slice a ragged path through her gossamer shields. She fell to the ground moments later as he laughed, drunk with the power this special blade gave him. The glory of the *Priori* would soon be his. He could taste it!

A noise from across the lot alerted him. Humans were coming around to claim their cars and he had to go. Pity, though. He would have liked to watch the woman die, but with such a wound as he'd just dealt, it wouldn't be long before she breathed her last. Vabian turned and walked away as if nothing of any importance had just occurred, while inside he crowed in triumph.

Mark Beauchamps, one of Betina's *were*coyote protectors found her in the parking lot when she failed to meet them at the prearranged time. She'd asked for some private time and he'd grudgingly agreed, though he'd watched her from across the street as she went into the local grocer, shopped, and then left the store. His partner was supposed to watch for her car. Only she never drove out of the parking lot.

She was out of their direct view for only about five minutes, but apparently that's all it took. Sending up the alarm when she didn't reappear in a reasonable time from behind the store, the *were*coyotes ran back there to check on her. They found her on the ground, near death from a gaping slice to her abdomen. Mark got on his cell phone, mobilizing the pack and alerting the prime alphas, Tim and Rafe, immediately.

Signaling for his partner to bring their truck around, Mark lifted Betina carefully into his arms, suppressing the need to howl out his rage and sorrow. He'd done this. He'd allowed it to happen and blood would be spilled to avenge this wrong. He vowed it with every fiber of his being. How he ached to follow the faint trail left by her attacker that very moment!

But for now he had to do all he could to save Betina's precious life. Healing her was beyond his meager skills, but perhaps the young priestess could do something. As the truck squealed to a halt in front of him, Mark climbed gingerly into the wide extended cab, cradling Betina's fragile body with his, holding her securely while his partner drove the distance to the prime alphas' home up the mountain. That's where the young priestess was.

The trip had never taken so long.

Allie met the truck with Tim and Rafe, as the *were*coyotes pulled up in front of their house only minutes later. She knew every *were* for miles around had been alerted or was in the process of being notified of the continued attacks on the women who were so precious to them. Priestesses were rare, Rafe had explained, and the alliance between them and all *were*, forged long ago, stood firm. It had to. For the safety and protection of all.

Clearing a path to the guest bedroom on the first floor, Allie swept back the covers as a tall, lean man she'd never met before carried Betina in. He treated her limp form with such gentle

157

care, and he reeked of such sorrow and guilt, Allie couldn't help but put a hand on his shoulder when he stepped back from the bed.

"It's okay." She tried to soothe the stranger, but his eyes were cold and dead as he looked from Betina to her.

"No, it's not." The man's gaze rose to Tim and Rafe, who were standing just behind her and the man dropped to his knees. "Forgive me, if you can. She asked for privacy and I gave it to her, even though I knew better. I'll never forgive myself."

"We'll sort this out later, Mark. Why don't you go out to the living room and tell everyone exactly what happened." Tim stepped forward and Allie moved to Betina's side, leaving the men to deal with each other. She knew by "everyone" Tim meant the collection of alphas who led the various tribes, packs and clans in the area. As before, they were all converging on her new home for what amounted to a war council.

Allie moved closer to Betty, looking carefully at the horrific wound and wondering just where to start. She'd never dealt with anything like this before and she was afraid she didn't have the skill to help her mentor. The older woman was paler than Allie had ever seen her, as if she were simply fading away. Allie reached out to touch the slashing, ragged wound on her abdomen and was shocked back by a powerful feeling of evil and dread.

Forcing her hands to move, Allie widened her stance and planted her feet firmly under herself before trying again. The malevolent force resisted her, pushing back against her outstretched hands, not allowing her near Betina's battered body.

"I need some help here. Whatever this is, it's pushing me back."

Rafe was instantly behind her, pushing forward with his chest against her back as she redoubled her efforts. Focusing her energy, she stabbed at the dark force, relying purely on instinct since her lessons hadn't progressed to cover anything remotely like this yet.

With one last significant thrust of her power, the black shield dissipated, fleeing before her light energies. Allie banished them to the earth, to be reabsorbed and not manifest again, as Betina had shown her. Now she saw the true extent of the wound and it made her sick inside.

"This was made with magic."

"Or magic directed through a blade. Probably the one that got me. I can smell the silver." Rafe's voice was thick with anger.

"You think that man Vabian did this?"

Rafe sighed heavily. "Who else?"

"What do I do?" Allie was scared, but Betty needed her.

"You've already begun," Tim spoke at her side, looking down at the pale woman in the bed. "Call upon the earth, call upon the Lady, call upon the creatures of land and sky. Use your inner eye to see where the tainted magic is and send it to ground. Let Gaia absorb it away so it can't hurt Betina anymore."

That sounded good, but Allie was at a loss as to just how to do it. Her confusion must've shown on her face as Rafe released her. Moving to her side, he smoothed back her hair with a reassuring half-smile.

"This is what you were born to do, Allie. The knowledge is within you. All you have to do is follow your instincts and focus on the goal."

"You make it sound so simple."

"It is simple." Tim took her other hand, capturing her attention. "It's fear that makes it complicated."

"Fight past the fear, Allie," Rafe soothed her, stepping back as Tim did the same. "Reach within. We'll be here to guard your back and stand for the *were*."

It was those last words that triggered a memory of the ceremony on Samhain. Betty had used similar words, calling on the various aspects of life that all served the Lady. Allie didn't know the words and didn't dare speak them aloud, but the intent was the important thing. Or so Betty had taught her.

Gathering the energies to her, she was surprised at the amount of power that came at her call. Never before had she felt such power at her command. She only hoped it was enough to save Betty.

Allie shaped the energy, strategizing the best way to dissipate the dark stain, spreading even now over Betina's bright soul. This magic wound was worse than any physical injury she suffered. This dark magic seeped into her soul, dimming its light and stealing its power. This was power twisted to evil purpose and only Allie could stand in its way and stop it before it stole Betina's spirit completely. That, was a fate worse than death.

At least in death there was transition. The soul lived on in different form—or so she believed. This though, was permanent death. Dissipation of the spirit, destruction of all that was Betty and all that would ever be. This fit Allie's definition of pure evil.

Calling on the Lady and the spirits of all those who served Her, Allie prayed for help as she gathered still more energy. The dark stain was strong and Allie didn't know if she had the skill yet to wield the energies—or enough power—to dissipate such darkness.

The power grew and still she waited. There was something missing, some ritual element she needed. Following her instincts, Allie stood on Betina's right side and extended her arms.

"Stand at her feet," she gasped out, containing the phenomenal build up of energy as her mates moved quickly to do her bidding. Something—or someone—was still missing. She could feel it. In a flash Allie remembered the glimpse she'd had of Betty's true nature during Rafe's healing and knew what she had to do.

"I stand for the Lady," she said simply, nodding to her mates as they watched her with concerned eyes. They knew their part. They'd performed it during the Samhain ceremony. She trusted they'd know what to do now.

"We stand for the *were,*" Tim said in a strong voice, holding his hands out to the side, containing the energy as Rafe did the same.

"And we stand for the creatures of sky and land," Rafe added, his eyes curious as he watched Allie.

"I call upon Betina's kin to join us here in this circle. Take up your place at her side, representative of the fey who would aid her." The twins' eyes widened as Allie spoke, but she felt the rightness of what she'd just done as the shift in magic communicated like a ripple across the small room and into realms beyond.

In a blinding flash of light, a man appeared across from her. He was tall, dark-haired, handsome, and dressed head to toe in fantastical, shining armor. This was a warrior from another realm, and though she'd never seen one before, she knew this was a Knight of the Fey.

"Welcome, Sir Knight."

"Who calls me to my cousin's side? And why is she in such dire straits?" The man's expression was both accusing and concerned, but Allie could see he had great affection for the little woman lying so still in the bed.

"I called you, sir, and as you can see, we don't have time right now to fill you in. Will you stand for the fey in our healing circle?"

The man straightened, looking measuringly at Tim and Rafe before nodding and raising his mail-clad hands.

"I stand for the fey warriors of the Forgotten Realms."

The circle snapped into place and the building pressure eased somewhat on Allie, though the energies continued to gather. She looked at the knight, catching the concern in his gaze.

"Will you help me wield these energies? I'm afraid I don't know what to do."

A brief smile flashed across his handsome face as he nodded. "I'm a warrior of the fey, priestess. I know how to fight this kind of magic."

Hallelujah! She'd done the right thing, she realized with a huge sigh of relief. She'd called a warrior who knew how to do what she couldn't.

"I can pass this energy to you," Allie thought aloud, relieved when the knight bowed his head.

"As it should be. The priestess is the nexus, the reservoir of strength. The rest of us are the weapons which defend and protect."

She felt the fey warrior harness the energies through the circle, relieving the pressure on her immeasurably, though still more energy flowed up from the earth into her and into the circle. In fascination she watched as he fashioned a sword of light from the swirling energy that, in his hands, became tangible. With the sword, he broke through the darkness that had once again surrounded Betina. Allie's circle encompassed it and forced it down into the earth to be reabsorbed and dissipated.

It took a long time, but the warrior fought through all the darkness until only light was left. The light of Betina's pure soul and the light from the remaining strength of the circle. All of them were haggard and trembling with strain when the final, clinging particles of darkness were finally done away with.

"Pull back now, Priestess," the fey warrior advised. "The job is done."

Allie used the last of her strength to do as the man said. She called back the circle and felt it snap apart at her command and then she felt herself falling. Only the fast reflexes of her *were* mate kept her from connecting sharply with the floor. Tim caught her in his arms as Rafe faced the strange knight, on guard.

But the knight wasn't paying any attention to them, Allie saw through weary eyes. His focus was on Betina as he sat gingerly on the bed at her side. Tim dragged a chair over and sat Allie down in it as if she were a rag doll. She was awake for the most part, but terribly drained and her muscles wouldn't support her.

"Who are you?" she asked the knight before she could censor her words.

The man looked up at her, pinning her with eyes the color of lilac blooms.

"I'm Duncan, half-fey warrior and cousin to Betina. Thank you for calling me. I would not wish to see her harmed."

"I'm Allie and these guys are Tim and Rafe." Allie's hand trembled as she raised it to indicate the two men who watched the fey knight with interest and just a hint of challenge. Alphas were always on guard, she realized.

Duncan nodded at them in turn. "Cousin Betina has mentioned you, lords of the *were* and your new mate. Congratulations on your joining." Her mates nodded, seeming a little more at ease with the strange man's knowledge and his actions so far. "Now will you tell me what happened? Who did this?"

"A *Venifucus* mage named Patrick Vabian. Or so we believe. He attacked us a few days ago, trying to get to Allie, aided by a vampire he'd duped into helping him. The only reason we're still alive is because the vampire took exception to being lied to and switched sides, helping us fight Vabian," Tim explained.

Rafe picked up the tale. "Every *were* in this territory and beyond has been searching for the bastard since, with no sign. Until today."

"Did she not have guards? I thought the alliance meant she would be protected by your people."

Tim growled low at the challenge, but Rafe stayed him.

"Of course she had guards."

"Then they are dead. I'm sorry for your loss." The knight bowed his head.

"They're not dead," Allie felt compelled to clarify.

"Then they soon will be!" A martial light came into the man's purple eyes as he stood and made for the door.

"Whoa, not so fast there, Lancelot." Rafe stopped the knight with two strong hands against the middle of his chest.

"I'm Duncan. Not Lancelot." The words were icy cold with anger and Allie made an effort to stand, causing all eyes to focus on her.

"We haven't heard the details yet of what occurred, but the man who brought her here took full responsibility. He's outside right now and I think we need to hear his story before we make any accusations."

After a tense moment where the men seemed to take each others' measure, the warrior stood down.

"You speak wisely, priestess."

"Call me Allie, please."

Duncan nodded formally.

"This is what we're going to do." Tim moved toward the door as well. "The three of us are going to go out into the living room and find out exactly what occurred today. Allie," he glanced over at her, "are you okay to stay with Betina?" When she nodded, he went on. "I'll send you some help from the females so you can clean her up a bit. She'll be unconscious for a while, right?" Tim's gaze shifted to the knight and the man nodded.

"She will probably be unconscious for several hours yet. It was a very deep wound."

"Okay then." Tim took one side of the fey warrior while Rafe took the other, flanking him and giving him little opportunity to launch any kind of attack in their home as they walked out the door, one after the other.

Allie sighed and rested her head back against the chair, starting when a few of the *were* women came in, waking her from the light doze she'd slipped into. They brought fragrant soapy water and soft cloths with them and set to work on cleaning up poor, battered Betina as best they could.

Chapter Ten

Tim watched the fey warrior carefully as they headed into the living room. The room went still long before they entered, every *were* gathered there aware of the strange, new, non-*were* scent in the house.

"Who's this?" Rocky asked the question clearly on everyone's mind as soon as they entered, the barrel-chested grizzly practically barring the way as he eyed the newcomer suspiciously. All eyes were on the three who entered, though several were watching all possible entries and exits, as it should be. *Were*folk were vigilant by nature. Alphas even more so, and this was the largest gathering of alphas in the region.

"I am Duncan the demi-fey, Knight of the Forgotten Realms. I came where called. Who challenges me?"

Every *were* in the room stood to face the stranger, making Tim proud, but he waved them off as Rafe supplied the details.

"He's Betina's cousin from the faerie realm. He popped in when Allie called and helped heal her."

"Then the High Priestess is alive?" This pained question came from the *were*coyote who'd brought her in.

"She's alive," Tim confirmed.

"But unwell," Duncan added, staring at the man who'd spoken. "It will be some time before she is fully healed."

Mark Beauchamps was a young alpha who'd taken control of his pack early. The former alpha had been shot by human hunters who took exception to his natural right to howl at the moon. Tim didn't know the man well, but he was fast earning his respect by taking responsibility for his actions, as he did again now. Mark walked right up to the fey warrior—still clad in full armor, which was a rather intimidating sight—and knelt before him, surprising them all.

"It was my fault." Mark's strong voice rang with remorse and anger, as well as bucketfuls of regret. "I let her go into the grocery store alone, though I watched from the street without her knowledge."

Rafe moved to Mark's side, but the knight stopped him from speaking with a raised hand.

"Rise, sir, and tell me the entire tale."

Clearly shaken, Mark rose and took a seat on the couch. All the other alphas were arrayed around him in the large room, the fey warrior still flanked by Tim and Rafe in case he made any sudden moves. Tim didn't quite trust the fey knight yet, regardless of what he'd done for Betina. Trust took time. And Betina was his acknowledged kin. His feelings toward her might not extend to her chosen allies, and Tim and Rafe had a responsibility to protect their people. If Mark were truly at fault, he would be dealt with. But by his fellow alphas. Not by this strange fey warrior.

"Sandy and I were with Betina all morning," the alpha coyote began. "We usually do the morning shift since Betina likes to go shopping with Sandy. But every once in a while Betina asks us to fall back and let her shop alone, and we usually let her, though we watch from the street unbeknownst to her."

"But you knew the threat had increased since the attack on Allie," Rafe's voice was tough with the shaken man.

"I knew it, but Betina's like an aunt to us. She wanted her privacy and I figured she'd be safe enough in a busy, public place. Sandy was covering the exit and had the car ready to follow Betina's once she hit the street. I watched the front door from across the street. We had every angle covered but one—the back parking lot. She was out of our sight for five minutes at most."

"Five minutes was all the time he needed," the knight commented harshly.

Mark hung his head, dragging his hands through his hair. "I know. Like I said, it was my decision. My fault."

The tall fey warrior moved forward, but Tim signaled his brother to hang back and see what the knight would do. Silence reigned for a long moment as the fey warrior looked down on the clearly distraught man. At length, the warrior sighed.

"I know my cousin well and I know how convincing she can be. Half-fey, she's not above using a touch of the Glamour to get her way, and I'm not surprised you gave in to her request. If you are to blame, I must also share part of this blame, for it was to visit me Underhill that she wished to be alone."

Mark looked up sharply at the fey warrior, his troubled eyes wide and lit with confusion. Tim saw the look of remorse cross the warrior's face before he took a seat on the sturdy coffee table and leaned his mail-clad elbows on his knees.

"She was only in the store for about ten minutes," Mark said quietly. "She didn't leave it."

"Yes, she did," the warrior responded. "Time works differently Underhill. Cousin Betina actually spent several hours visiting with me before retreating back whence she'd come."

"How is that possible?" Mark looked totally confounded.

Rafe stepped forward. "You're saying our Betina's half-fey? Like you are?"

The warrior nodded and Tim could guess what had happened.

"We never knew she was half-fey. Betina kept that a secret even from us. Can I assume that flash of light when you appeared at her bedside is the way you—or she—would travel from one dimension to another?" Again the knight nodded. "Then her watchers would most definitely notice it, unless she did it in just the right place, away from their eyes and unable to be scented."

"The rest room. The grocery store has a one-seater," Ryan supplied helpfully from across the room.

"With a good sturdy lock on the door," someone else piped in.

"So it's a safe bet that our Betina ducked into the rest room, poofed out to another dimension, had tea with you," Rafe nodded toward the knight, "then poofed back into the rest room a few moments later, with none the wiser—especially not her *were* guardians."

"Who knew she had it in her?" Rocky asked with a chuckling growl.

"Does she do this often?" Rafe asked.

Duncan nodded once more. "We're closer than most Underhill because we're both half-human and therefore not well accepted. She misses her family there, and though she's chosen this path of exile, she visits me every once in a while. She and my father were very close in the old days and I think she feels some responsibility for me even now."

"Okay, so let's go through this step by step. But first..." Tim looked to Rocky, the *de facto* leader when the twins were busy elsewhere, based sheerly on his size and standing with all *were*. No one messed with a *were*bear. Especially a three hundred pound grizzly. "You sent a group of trackers out already, right?"

"Yeah, for all the good it will do us. That mage has tricks we've never seen before. He can mask his scent and practically doesn't leave a trail at all, for as loud and clumsy as you say he was in the woods."

"He masks his passage magically," Duncan said quickly. "I may be of some help there. I have the flavor of his power now after seeing what he did to my cousin. I'd like to see the area where the attack took place. I don't expect he's still nearby, but I may garner a clue that could lead us to him elsewhere."

"Good idea, but you can't walk around town dressed as you are." Rafe chuckled as the knight looked down at his armor. With a flash of his magic, the armor disappeared to be replaced by jeans and a white button-down shirt much like the one Tim wore.

"Holy shit," Rocky swore, breaking the silence. Such a casual display of fey magic was not something one saw every day.

Duncan laughed as he looked at the stunned faces around the room. "One use of the Glamour." He shrugged. "Will this do?"

Tim nodded. "Suits me. Just don't do anything like that in public. Humans aren't used to magic and we like to keep a low profile."

Duncan nodded though an amused sparkle lit his strangely colored eyes. "I have been in your world before you know. My mother raised me here, though it's been some time since I was last able to come through."

"Why's that?" Rafe asked.

"Queen Mab trapped me Underhill. She quarreled with my father and banished me to a small corner of her realm. I could receive visitors, but I couldn't leave—until your young priestess called me with her power. Her call was stronger than the enchantment that held me, with the Lady's power behind it."

"Shit!" Rafe eyed the knight. "You mean Allie managed a prison break?"

Duncan laughed outright. "I'm not a criminal. More like a political exile, if you must have a comparison. I'm just as glad to be here in this realm. I never much liked Underhill, but my father is there and I used to go visit him. Mab didn't like that because I'm half-human and she blew the slightest disagreement into a huge to-do, banishing me to the Isle of Nevermore." He just laughed at the suspicious looks all the other men were giving him. "Don't worry. Cousin Betina will tell you I'm no villain when she wakes. In the meantime," his face grew serious, "we must find her attacker and bring justice to him."

"Well, we agree on that at least."

"Do you have a horse I could borrow?"

A few of the men laughed, but Rafe slapped the knight on the back. "We've got something even better than horses to get where we're going. Just how long has it been since you've visited our world?"

Duncan appeared to think on that. "Several hundred years have passed here, I would think."

Tim realized this man had probably missed the industrial revolution completely. He still expected to get around on horseback and was even now looking around at the modern furnishings with questions in his startlingly purple eyes.

"You're in for some big surprises then, Duncan." Tim led the way to the door. Duncan followed with Rafe right behind him. They'd have to watch over this stranger in a strange land for their own protection—and his.

For one thing, Tim didn't think Betina wouldn't take kindly to her allies letting harm come to her cousin. There was also the secrecy of their existence. If this rogue knight from the faerie realm started letting loose with magic in front of regular mortals, it would be hard to quell the uproar and continue to hide in plain sight among them.

Even though a good percentage of the people who lived in the area were *were*folk, there were still quite a few humans who liked to live close to nature, and tourists coming through all the time on the way to the national park. Someone would have to watch over Duncan until he learned the lay of the land and what was, and was not, acceptable behavior for a magic user in the mortal realm.

As predicted, Duncan was duly impressed with the monstrous black beast Tim called a "truck" as they sped downhill to the small town where Betina had been attacked. As they approached the town, the knight craned his neck to see the odd things all around him.

Rafe pulled into the parking lot and parked near the edge so they could all get a good look at the entire area. Duncan immediately sensed the wrongness in the air when he stepped out of the truck. The scent of dark magic lingered, as did the echoes of horror.

Duncan moved forward unerringly to the spot where Betina had been assaulted. A glance at the young *were*coyote who had accompanied them in the extended cab of the truck confirmed his suspicions. The *were*folk were smart enough to leave him be while he surveyed the area on both a physical and magical level.

Duncan bent to pick up a small stick—seeming of no importance to human or even *were*—but to a mage, it was the key link in a complex spell of warding. It was what had hidden Betina's attacker from even her sharp senses, until the villain was ready to spring. Worse, it was brand of magic he knew well. It reeked of fey power.

"The world has changed greatly in the time I've been Underhill, but one thing remains the same." The *were*folk gathered round Duncan as he stared off into the distance, anger building in him at this discovery.

"And what's that?" Rafe asked.

"Treachery." Sneering, Duncan snapped the twig in his hand and the small array of leaves and acorns on the ground were consumed in a flash of fire from which the *were* fell back. "That charm was of fey design. No mortal mage should have this knowledge. It is too dangerous."

"Then one of your kind is in league with the *Venifucus*." Tim spoke the name Duncan dreaded to hear.

"*Venifucus?* Are you sure?"

The alphas nodded. "We believe the mage who attacked Allie, and now Betina, is *Venifucus*. He claimed to be *Altor Custodis* according to Dante, but his actions prove otherwise."

"Who is this Dante?"

"A vampire," Tim answered. "He helped the mage attack Allie at first, then when he realized he'd been used, he fought against the mage with us. His name is Dante d'Angleterre."

"I knew him." Duncan recalled the bloodletter he'd known briefly. "He was a good man when I knew him."

"I believe he still is. He proved himself a man of honor when he helped drive the mage away." Tim's voice rang with surety.

Duncan nodded. "He will be of help in this hunt. I fear the enemy has many advantages over your kind this time, but having attacked my cousin, I am now obligated to bring justice to this villain. I will help you, if you'll accept my aid."

Rafe smiled grimly. "Right now I think we need all the help we can get."

Betina was awake when the men returned from their tracking. The trail, as expected, petered out just beyond the parking lot and even Duncan's magical senses could not detect where the mage had gone. Rafe used the ride back to fill Duncan in on the facts they knew so far. He went into detail about the attack on Allie and what little they knew about their prey, the mage Patrick Vabian.

Duncan was angry, Rafe could see easily enough, and upset by the idea that one of his fey brethren could be aiding the *Venifucus*. Rafe took it as a good sign, knowing that if their enemies were using such powerful magics, they'd need the same kinds of skills in their fight against them.

When they reached the homestead, Rocky and the rest of the alphas who'd remained behind greeted them. A veritable army of *were* guarded every approach to the house and the woods for miles around. No one would get past them all. No one would harm the precious priestesses inside the house ever again. Not if they had anything to say about it.

When the three men entered the guest room, Betina was sitting up in the large bed, still pale, but her color was a little better. Allie was seated in a chair at her bedside.

"Duncan," Betina said softly, "it's good to see you in this realm. I see you've met my friends and allies."

Duncan moved to sit on the side of the bed, taking Betina's hands in his. "You chose your allies well, dear cousin." Allie was seated near him and he reached out for one of her hands. "I owe you a great debt, priestess, for freeing me from my exile."

"Betina filled me in on where you were. I'm glad you were freed, but I can't really take any credit for it. I called on the Lady and Betina's kin. You were what She sent me." Allie blushed a bit as she explained.

"Nevertheless," Duncan was polite, but it seemed he would not be denied, "it was your call that summoned me, your power and that of the Lady you serve which freed me. If you have need of anything from me, it is yours." The knight brought Allie's hand to his lips and sealed his promise with a kiss.

Tim growled low in his throat and Rafe felt the same possessiveness over their mate, but he also suspected the fey knight was a man of honor and meant nothing but respect by the gesture. Still it rankled, and Rafe couldn't help but move next to Allie's chair, lifting her hand from the knight's and tucking it close to his side. It was a clear statement of ownership and though Allie blushed at the possessive stance, Duncan nodded politely and turned back to his cousin.

"Dear cousin, I have bad news. We inspected the location of your attack and I found traces of an Elspian Ring."

Betina paled even further, if such a thing were possible. "You dismantled it?"

"Of course. Such a thing should not be left lying around."

"Then—"

"I'm afraid so."

"Would somebody please interpret for the non-fey in the room?" Rafe smiled politely as he made the request, though he could see the frustration on Tim's face.

Betina sighed long and hard. "Dear boys, I've been hiding amongst you for so long. Can you forgive me?"

Tim surprised his brother by stepping forward. Rafe moved to the older woman's other side, mirroring his brother's stance.

"We all have secrets, Betina. Some bigger than others." Tim glanced wryly at the knight seated at her side.

"There's nothing to forgive, milady," Rafe said softly, stroking her hand with fondness. In truth, she was like a mother to him and his brother, regardless of how young she looked. She'd always looked the same, as long as they'd known her—and that was a long time indeed. It all made sense now, of course. If she wasn't immortal, she was damn close to it.

"The time for secrets is over at any rate," Duncan said softly. "The presence of an Elspian Ring in this realm is a bad sign of things to come, I fear."

"What is it?" Allie asked, her voice strong although Rafe knew she had to be feeling the same apprehension they all felt at the knight's dire tone.

"It's nothing to look at unless you have certain magics at your disposal," Betina said softly. "To a human it would look like nothing more than a bit of debris on the ground. But if they unwittingly stepped through it, dire consequences could result, depending on what the mage who cast it intended."

"The one I found near the scene of your attack was almost certainly used to hide the attacker's presence. It was crude, but expertly done."

"So the human mage cast it, but he had been taught well," Betina thought aloud.

Duncan nodded. "Or cast it often enough, over time, to gain such skill."

"So that's how he's been masking his presence from us?" Tim asked. "This Elspian Ring is strong enough to foul *were* senses?"

"Most certainly." Duncan nodded grimly. "It can muddle any being's sense whether physical or magical. It will work equally well on any dweller of this realm, and most from Underhill."

"But not Duncan," Betina said with a hint of pride. "Oh, the Lady knew what She was doing when She sent you to us, cousin."

Duncan bowed his head respectfully but said nothing to the compliment.

"Why doesn't it affect him?" Allie wanted to know.

To this the knight objected somewhat. "Oh no, priestess, the Elspian Ring would affect me just as easily as anyone else were I to unwittingly cross it, but my magical gift is such that it allows me to sense and avoid the darker magics—and this kind of ring is among the darkest of all. It was first created by the murderess Elspia, hence its name. She perfected and used it over many years to do her foul deeds, killing many beings, both magical and mundane, in many realms. There has never been a more evil woman known to our realm."

"It was her son, Lachlan, who founded the *Venifucus* in ancient times," Betina said, some of her strength returning along with her anger.

"You're saying Elspia was fey? And this Lachlan—was he fey as well?"

"Only half. Like me." Duncan replied. "His father was a human of this realm, murdered by Elspia not long after impregnating her."

"So did he inherit his mother's magical abilities?" Allie stood and started to pace as she grew agitated.

Duncan shrugged. "Unfortunately yes. She taught him all she knew. But he didn't survive much past founding the *Venifucus*. He was tried in the faerie realm for crimes he'd committed against Queen Mab and sentenced to banishment in the Farthest Realm."

"And where's that? Someplace worse than the Isle of Nevermore?" Rafe asked only half joking.

But Duncan was dead serious as he responded. "Infinitely worse. It is comparable to your legends of hell, and it is said there is no return from that realm. Once you are sent there, you never come back. Queen Mab has sent many there over the eons. I'm lucky she didn't send me there as well."

"She wouldn't dare!" Betina's color was high and her voice shook with anger. Duncan leaned close to her, rubbing her trembling shoulder with obvious care.

"Calm yourself, cousin. You know she would not dare your anger or my father's. I'm safe enough for now, here in this realm. Perhaps I'll share your exile with you?" His smile coaxed the older woman to calm down.

"You can't go back anytime soon, Duncan. She'll know by now that you've escaped."

"Then I'll stay here, with you. Besides, it is obviously the Lady's will. She sent me to you when any number of other fey would gladly have come to your aid. You still have many friends and supporters Underhill, dear cousin. I'm just one of many."

"Apparently," Allie turned from her pacing to appraise the knight, "you're the one we need."

Again Duncan bowed his head in acknowledgement. "Apparently so, Priestess."

They talked for a bit more, but before long Betina grew tired and Allie suggested they adjourn the discussion to the living room. Betina was a great source of knowledge but apparently priestesses rarely engaged in battle. In this case, Allie realized, Duncan would be of far more help in planning strategy and analyzing the possible strengths and weaknesses of their foe.

The war council in the living room resumed and Allie took her place between her mates. If any sort of battle plan was being constructed, she wanted in on it. Allie had a personal score to settle with Vabian for the way he'd hurt Rafe and Betty. She didn't care if priestesses didn't fight. She'd show them all a thing or two. She might not be as quick or strong as some of these male *were*, but she had magic on her side. She'd faced Vabian before and been of some help in protecting Rafe. She knew she could help now, no matter how much the twins wanted to keep her safe and coddled indoors where no harm would come to her. They didn't quite realize it yet, but they'd have a fight on their hands if they tried to keep her out of this one.

"We need to get him out in the open. In the woods, where our strengths are greatest," Rocky said from his habitual position near the doorway leading to the kitchen.

"But if he's using this ring thing to hide from our senses, he'll have the advantage no matter what the setting," one of the others pointed out.

"Not necessarily," Duncan said, rising to stand near the fireplace. "I may be able to show you signs to look for. Humans would probably not be able to see such, but you are *were*, you have advantages. Some of you might be able to recognize signs of the Elspian Ring that are too subtle for human senses." He bent to pick a few twigs and ash out of the fireplace, then moved to the large, central coffee table. "The Elspian Ring is not a perfect circle. It has several dips and curves, like so."

Duncan arranged the twigs and ash in an odd pattern that almost resembled the outline of a jigsaw puzzle piece, but not quite so regular. It looked totally random to Allie, but then she saw the flare of power as the ends of the ring joined. She jumped up from her seat on the sofa, unconsciously erecting a shield as she moved to encompass Tim and Rafe in her sphere of protection.

"Be at ease, young priestess," Duncan stood to face her. "This is not the Elspian Ring, but a mere facsimile for training purposes. I would never call such darkness into your home."

"Disperse it, Duncan. Now." Allie felt uneasy with the humming energy so near the twins, though they seemed totally unaware of it.

Duncan shrugged and picked up the linking twig, snapping it in his hands as the rest of the arrangement disappeared in a puff of smoke.

"Forgive me for distressing you, Priestess."

Allie stood back, but didn't sit down. Rafe and Tim were eyeing her strangely, but ready to leap to her defense should she need it.

"None of you guys saw that? Or felt it? Or heard it?" Allie could barely believe it. "It hummed with power! And glowed. It crackled against my skin like static electricity."

Tim and Rafe shook their heads, eyes narrowed on the fey warrior.

"That's because you are a Sensitive. Many priestesses have the skill, but you are new to it. Soon you will be able to differentiate between harmless callings like the one I just performed and those more sinister. Even now, I believe you would feel the innate evil in the Elspian Ring should you come into contact with the real thing." Duncan bowed his head to her in a formal show of respect. "You will be of great use to us in this battle, Priestess."

"Call me Allie, please."

Rafe and Tim stood, towering over her. "She's not going anywhere near this battle, Duncan," Tim said hotly.

"She's Vabian's target and we're not giving him another clear shot at her," Rafe added.

"Now just hold on a minute." Allie knew this battle was coming but she would have preferred to fight it in private. Fate, apparently, had other plans. "I can help. I stood against him before. My shield held and kept Rafe alive until help could arrive. I don't think I'm as vulnerable to this Vabian guy as you seem to think I am."

"Oh, lady," Duncan broke in from behind her, "you are more vulnerable than any in this room to Patrick Vabian's magic."

Rafe and Tim both raised their eyebrows at her as if to say, "See?"

"But then, you are also probably the best equipped to fight him. Aside from myself, of course."

An uproar was avoided only by a loud knock on the front door. All eyes flew to Rafe and Tim for direction. Allie knew no one could approach this house without one of the many *were* on guard outside noticing and alerting them well beforehand, but no such warning had come.

Tim got up and went to the door, Rafe staying with Allie and placing her behind him. Allie looked around his wide shoulders to see what was going on as Tim opened the door.

The vampire had come to call.

"May I come in?" Dante asked with a hint of a smile.

Darkness had fallen outside while the war council deliberated over what to do. The room was stunned to silence, suspicion and distrust crossing many a face as they all watched the vampire. Duncan moved swiftly toward the door.

"Be sure of him before inviting him in, for once invited in, a bloodletter can enter at will." Duncan faced the vampire, standing next to Tim in the doorway, practically blocking Allie's view completely, but she could see the look of surprise cross the vampire's eyes, followed by what looked like a genuine smile. "It's been a long time, my old friend."

"Too long, Duncan. You look well. I thought you were long dead."

"Exiled, I'm afraid. Held prisoner these many years Underhill by Auntie Mab's decree."

"Bummer."

Duncan cocked his head at the modern expression but let it pass.

"Have you changed allegiances in the years I've not seen you?" the knight asked formally. "Be warned, I will still recognize a falsehood from truth."

Dante smiled and shook his head. "My interests have always been mainly in keeping myself happy and comfortable, but I've no love for the *Venifucus*. That has never changed. What I did, I did out of ignorance and laziness. I've come back here to make amends, if possible, and seek my promised justice."

Duncan seemed to consider his words then finally nodded. "It's good to know some things never change. If these *were* will not have you for a fighting companion, I will take your aid, Dante, for the mage you set loose here has now injured one of my kin whom I love dearly. He must pay for that insult."

Dante looked truly angry, his eyes flashing red in the uncertain light from outside. "I'm truly sorry, my old friend. Vabian will die for duping me. Whether this wolf invites me in or not."

Duncan nodded and moved back. That left just Tim facing the vampire in the doorway.

"Well, what'll it be?" Dante's voice rang with boredom, but his eyes flashed challenge.

Tim seemed to consider. "Did you bring back my bike?"

Dante tossed Tim the keys with a grin. "Gassed her up too. Thanks for the loan. You'll find her parked at the first bend in the road downhill, behind the large oak."

"Do I have your word you won't prey on any of the *were* in this area? That you won't take *were* blood?"

Dante grinned, showing his fangs, now recessed at rest, but still slightly visible. "Not unless they offer."

"That's good enough for me." Tim stepped back from the door, opening it wide. "Please come in, Dante. We could really use your help."

Chapter Eleven

"I want to do this," Allie argued hours later. They'd arrived at the idea of using some sort of bait to lure the magic user into their trap, but Allie was the only thing they could think of that he might want badly enough to try for.

"No way in hell." Tim stood firm against her, backed by his twin and a whole bunch of other angry alpha *were*.

"It's the only way to get Vabian where you need him."

"We'll find another way."

"There is no other way!" Frustration made anger spark up and down her arms. Unbeknownst to her, she was sending little electrical shocks throughout the room.

"Lady." Duncan stepped forward, putting a hand on her shoulder. She immediately felt some of the restless energy drain away from her. "Calm yourself. This does you no good."

"Don't. Touch. Her." Rafe stalked forward, surprising the heck out of Allie. He was usually the more affable of the twins, but apparently he'd had enough as he yanked her away from the fey knight and wrapped one arm around her middle. It was a possessive move that spoke volumes to all the dominant males in the room. Her independent nature demanded she fight against such barbaric behavior, but the newly discovered submissive side of her liked it all too much. Torn, she decided to say nothing.

Fighting his possessive stance in a room full of angry *were* was not a good idea. Plus, she didn't want to shame him or hurt his feelings. If Rafe was this close to the edge of his control, she could only imagine how Tim was holding it together. She'd go along for now, but when she got them alone, she'd have a thing or two to say.

"That's it. We're done for tonight." Dante stood across the room as he tossed aside the topographical map of the area they'd been using. "I must go soon at any rate."

They all knew what that meant. Dawn was approaching and the vampire had to hide from the sun. An uncomfortable stillness settled over the room.

"I will go with you." Duncan rose and started for the door but Dante stopped him.

"No, old friend. I must feed."

Again silence reigned, all eyes shifting to the vampire with uneasy suspicion, but Duncan continued forward.

"Of course you must. And if you are to be of any help against Vabian, you must feed from me."

Even Dante looked upset by this idea. "You've got to be kidding!"

"Not so, old friend. We need every weapon in our arsenal against the Elspian Ring. You, most of all."

"But—" Dante's face went even paler, if that were possible. "How can you trust me? How can I trust myself?"

"What exactly is going on here?" Tim demanded.

Duncan sighed as he turned back to the room. "Fey blood is deadly to vampires. It is simply too potent. But half-fey...now that is another matter. It can convey power to the vampire the likes of which few of their kind ever achieve, but since there are so few half-fey and we have rather formidable defenses of our own, it is something few bloodletters have ever tried."

"What will it do to him?" Allie felt worry in her heart for the creature who had saved them just days before.

Duncan shrugged. "It could kill him. Or it will make him the most powerful vampire on this earth—for a time. He will have the echoes of my magic at his command and I'm hoping it will enable him to detect the Elspian Ring. We know he fell prey to it before, else he would not have helped Vabian."

"You can't trust me with such power."

"I can, and I do. Unless you're much changed from the soul I knew centuries ago, you are the only vampire I would give such trust. And I knew many of your kind once upon a time." Duncan took Dante by the arm and led him to the door. "Besides, I will be connected to you, Dante. I'll know where you are and what you are doing at all times. Should you be tempted to stray, I'll end you without second thought."

"That's comforting." Dante allowed himself to be led outdoors. Tim followed, as did Rafe, still holding Allie in one tight arm.

"I hope you know what you're doing." Tim's message was stern and gruff to the half-fey knight.

Duncan nodded as Tim tossed him the keys to his truck. He then handed them to Dante, who at least knew how to drive.

"I have to believe this is the reason I was sent. This feels like the right path to me and I will follow it. Perhaps together, we can come up with some other plan than the one which puts your beautiful mate in such danger."

Allie tugged against Rafe's hold but it was no use. "I'm not afraid."

"I know you aren't, Priestess, and your courage does you credit, but you are too precious to put at risk." He would have touched her face but Rafe tugged her away with a growl. "Unless there is no other choice." Duncan eyed both twins sharply before climbing into the passenger side of the truck. Dante pulled off onto the road, spinning gravel, definitely upset, judging by the way he drove.

Tim hitched his chin at two of the alphas. "Have them followed and watched. Keep the perimeter secure, and get some rest. We reconvene after lunch."

With a final order, Tim took Allie's other arm and led her inside, straight to the big master bedroom. Even once they were alone, Rafe didn't let her go. She'd never seen him so intense. He growled low in his throat every time she moved, pulling her closer and closer.

"Rafe, you're holding me too tight. Ease up a bit, huh?"

He growled again, burying his face in her hair, but his arm around her waist eased only a little. It was as if he was beyond reason.

Tim's arms came around both of their shoulders.

"Easy, brother."

"I won't put her in danger deliberately."

"No," Tim agreed. "We'll find another way."

"There is no other way. We have to lure Vabian out and I'm the perfect bait."

Rafe just stared, anger clear in his every line as Tim came around to face her, standing close, but not touching her.

"We can't." Tim ran a hand through his hair, dislodging the sun-kissed strands. "Allie, it goes against everything we are to deliberately put you in danger. Don't ask it of us. We just can't do it."

"Is that why you went all growly on me?" She turned to face Rafe, bringing one hand up to cup his jaw, noting the muscle ticking there as he tried to control his baser impulses.

"I don't like his hands on you."

"Who? Duncan?" Rafe's hands tightened as he searched deep in her eyes. She guessed he was looking for some sign she was attracted to the fey warrior, but though he was gorgeous, he did nothing for her. Her two wolves were all she needed in the world, and it was time they understood that.

"Rafe," Allie reached up and kissed him softly on the lips, "I love you. Duncan touched me to help dissipate some of the energy build-up...like a ground wire or something. He helped it drain away before I accidentally hurt somebody. I'm so new to this, I can't control the energy very well. He knows that and he was helping me without making it too obvious. He was saving me embarrassment in front of your friends. It was a nice gesture."

"Looked a little too 'nice' from where I was standing, Allie." Tim came up on her other side as Rafe finally let her go, only so she could be captured by his brother's strong arm. "We don't like other males touching you. For any reason." Tim sighed as he rested his forehead against hers. "It's our nature to be possessive. Please try to understand."

She cupped his stubbly cheeks and kissed him softly. "I think I do understand, but Duncan was only helping. I don't have any feelings for him in any way, other than maybe a little gratitude. Tim, I love *you*. Both of you."

"I think we need to prove it." Tim's gaze turned hot as he moved her toward the bed.

She didn't fear anything these men had up their sleeves. Well, not much anyway. She loved them and was coming to terms with that idea in her mind. She also loved what they did to her sexually. She'd never been so open or free with any man in her life before—much less two men at once. It was liberating.

"What did you have in mind?"

Rafe stood near the top of the bed, looking her over critically. "We know she likes her discipline," he said to his brother as if she weren't even there, "but what about a little bondage?"

Allie felt her pulse sputter with excitement as Rafe pulled a pair of handcuffs from behind his back. Tim rumbled his agreement as he pushed her forward, closer to the bed.

"Strip," he ordered and Allie felt her pussy contract with excitement at the order.

She complied, but didn't move too quickly. She wanted her men to enjoy this little striptease as much as she did. Slowly, her hands stroked over her own curves before undoing the fastenings and sliding the fabric away, layer by layer. She watched their reactions as her own breath sped in her chest. The fire in their eyes leapt as each part of her was bared, until finally, when she was completely naked, Rafe sprang.

He tackled her gently, pushing her back onto the bed and arranging her limbs to suit himself. Holding her gaze, he raised first one wrist, then the other upward, clicking the cuffs he'd positioned over one rung of the carved wooden headboard around her wrists softly. He made sure they wouldn't hurt her, checking the fit twice. The care he showed for her comfort reassured her, even as the feeling of helplessness before these two primitive warriors fired her senses.

She loved the way they looked at her. She loved everything about them, even if their incredibly possessive tendencies did annoy her at times. It was at times like these—when they were alone together—when the possessiveness thrilled her and made her want to be owned wholly and completely by both of these amazing men.

Tim sat down on the bed next to her, Rafe on her other side. He stroked his hand over her breast as if weighing the soft globe, pinching her nipple with deliberate motions while he pondered her.

"You let another man touch you," he accused. "You made Rafe angry. For that matter, you made me angry. Other men are not to touch what's ours. Is that clear?"

He squeezed her nipple, making her writhe in pleasure.

"Yes!"

Tim removed his hand. "Yes, what?"

Allie's gaze shot up to his. "Yes...Master."

His indulgent smile rewarded her as his hand moved back to her body, sloping down the curve of her waist to the curls at the juncture of her thighs. He patted her there, as if in approval.

"Good girl." His voice purred in her ear as he bent and licked her neck, making her shiver.

"But she still needs to be punished," Rafe reminded them both as Tim sat up, removing his hands.

"You're right, brother."

Allie looked over to Rafe and gasped. He held a small flogger with a myriad of soft strands at its tip that she'd never seen before.

"Like it?" He trailed the soft tresses over her trembling tummy. "I got it just for you, Allie."

Allie's mouth was too dry to answer. She could only stare at the amused deviltry in Rafe's eyes and the heat reflected there from the fire raging between them. She nodded once, her head whirling as Tim flipped her over. The chain holding the handcuffs together was long enough to accommodate the new position without putting too much stress on her wrists, but the added tension excited her.

Tim stuffed a pillow under her hips, raising them as Rafe smoothed his hand all over her curves, warming them, preparing her for what he might do next. Tim made sure she was comfortable, turning her head so she couldn't see Rafe, could only feel whatever he chose to do next. Tim held her gaze as he quickly undressed and came down beside her on the bed. He leaned up on one elbow so he could easily watch his brother and her expression at the same time.

She realized this was for Rafe. Something about the way Duncan had touched her had set off primitive instincts inside Rafe and this was all about calming him, making him secure in the knowledge that she was his. Tim was always so controlled, but of the two, he seemed to understand better that Allie was theirs completely. Rafe still needed proof and this was one way of proving her devotion to them. She'd do anything for them and was more than willing to prove it in any way they wanted. She trusted them. They were her mates.

"He loves you as much as I do," Tim whispered in her ear, biting the lobe just slightly in the way she loved.

"I know," she whispered back.

Tim pulled back, smiling softly down at her before he kissed her deep and slow. At the same time, Rafe's palms cupped her ass, massaging and kneading the soft skin, delving between lightly, prodding her sensitive hole. Tim pulled back after a long moment, leaving her feeling drugged. These two men affected her like no single man ever had before.

A second later, Rafe brought the flogger down on her ass, making her yelp in surprise more than pain. The soft threads of the flogger didn't really hurt so much as sting and the sting faded quickly into a pleasure she couldn't quite understand. She only knew she wanted more.

Tim watched her carefully, nodding over at his brother, apparently pleased with what he saw in her expression. He kissed her cheek as he moved back to watch the spectacle.

Rafe peppered her backside with soft strokes and hard strokes, long and short, on the fleshy part of her ass and down her thighs, even up her back, but he didn't hurt her. Not really. No, the little stings faded together into one long caress, though Allie wouldn't have believed it just a few moments before. His expert hands turned something that could easily have been painful and humiliating into one long full-body caress. Every stroke spoke of his love—and his possession. This was an eloquent statement of ownership and Allie writhed in the pleasure of knowing she belonged to Rafe, and to Tim, fully. So fully, in fact, she could give them full control of her fulfillment, trusting them to know best how to please her, even if she didn't quite know that herself.

Tim sat up, his hands stroking her ass, which was surely pink by now from the stimulation of the flogger, and pulled her cheeks apart with skillful fingers. She was so close to completion, even that little attention threatened to throw her over the edge. She heard fabric rustling, then felt Rafe come down beside her. His skin was hot against hers where he brushed close.

The nightstand drawer opened and closed and then more movement as Rafe sat across from Tim, his hand gliding over her backside. He smacked her with an open palm, making her wiggle her hips in excitement.

"You like that, don't you?" Tim asked. "Yes, we know you do." He smacked the other cheek with even more force and she moaned. "Rafe has never fucked your ass, Allie. I think it's time that changed. He needs you, sweetheart, as much as I do."

Tim spread her butt cheeks and she felt cool wetness drop down on her sensitive, overheated skin just before Rafe's big fingers swept down the crack of her ass, swirling the moisture and dipping just briefly inside the tight hole there. She gasped. They hadn't tried to take her at the same time since that first joining.

"We don't do this often, but every once in a while..." Tim massaged her ass as he leaned closer and bit one buttock with strong teeth, undoubtedly marking her. "Every once in a while, we need it like we need to breathe."

Rafe growled, apparently beyond speech at this point, and bent to bite her other cheek, even harder than Tim had. Rafe was almost beyond control, she sensed, but he was still careful with her, still unable to truly hurt her. She trusted him, trusted his instincts, trusted his love.

A moment later, she felt him move over and behind her, widening her legs with his knees before Tim spread her again, poking the tip of a bottle of lube up into her. A cool sensation spread through her a moment before she heard Rafe's growl and saw the small tube go flying across the room out of the corner of her eye. He was pretty far gone, but she knew he would never hurt her. Tim moved back up to her head, his gaze holding hers as he tried to reassure her, but she needed no reassurances. She loved these men. She knew they wouldn't hurt her, no matter how worked up they became. Hurting her would hurt them, and they could never deliberately hurt her, any more than she could consciously hurt one of them. They were joined. They were one.

Rafe's fingers speared up into her, causing a shiver of delight to pass through her entire body. He stilled and she knew on some level he was waiting to see if the shiver was of pleasure or fear. She made an effort to twist her body so she could see his face. If she contorted her spine, she just could.

"Come into me now, Rafe. Do it now."

She flopped back down, unable to hold the awkward position, but Tim was there to ease her way. His strong arms supported her and guided her, his eyes watching her bound hands carefully to see she came to no harm.

She got her knees under her a little and pushed up, offering herself blatantly to the man at her back. Rafe's growl preceded his advance and a moment later she felt the tip of his cock pushing steadily into the place he needed to go. The place she needed him. She breathed deeply as she fought to accept him, pushing out when she felt the need and sighing in pleasure when he was fully seated.

How she loved this man!

But the twins weren't done with her yet. Moving carefully, still seated fully in her ass, Rafe rolled with her to the side, untwisting the handcuff chain a quarter turn and giving her a little more leeway. Tim pulled the pillows away and sent them sailing to the floor as he moved in close. Lifting her top leg over his hips, he shoved his hard cock up into her pussy, pushing steadily as her body welcomed him with only a little difficulty. She felt so full, so warm, so loved. This was what she'd been missing. This was what she needed, just as much as she could feel their need. Now they were truly one.

She accepted them both into her body and then they began to move. Rafe pulled out, then moved back in as Tim echoed his movements in counterpoint. No matter what she did, she was filled, never left wanting, always a part of the men she loved.

Just the thought made her cry out in completion, but the spasms that wracked her body went on and on, unlike anything she'd ever experienced before. It was a little scary, but Tim was there, his warm eyes and his tender, loving hands as he kissed her. Rafe was behind her, nibbling on her shoulder, licking her neck in reassurance as she clenched and writhed on them both.

"It's okay, love," Tim whispered, settling his mouth under one of her ears, taking the opposite side of her neck as his brother. She knew what was coming next and they didn't disappoint.

Both men bit down on the cords of her neck as they thrust home, faster, more sure now than they had been, as her body became one long, hot, writhing orgasm. Their teeth where sharp and broke the skin just slightly, but she felt no pain. Only pleasure lit her being from within, shining her up into the atmosphere and back down again, caught safe in her lovers' embrace. God, how she loved them!

She felt them come simultaneously within her, filling her, driving her higher still as the pleasure went incredibly on. It was like nothing before and she knew she could never part from these two men. They were her life. They were her future. They were all that mattered.

"I love you both so much!" she cried, tears falling down her face as the beauty of the moment overwhelmed her completely. "I love you, I love you, I love you." Her voice floated softly on the winds of pleasure as she chanted their names and her love for them both.

Her men were filling her, their teeth marking her, their tongues lapping up her essence, and they heard every word in their hearts.

Rafe especially needed to hear her complete loss of control and her surrender to them. He'd needed that reassurance and now he had it, deep in his heart, in his soul. He would never doubt her again—or his own power to please her, to love her...to keep her.

He eased within her, but was unwilling to leave her body just yet. He licked the last of her blood away from his lips, knowing he hadn't really hurt her, but the need to mark her was inborn. Wolves didn't need blood like vampires did to live, but blood was a powerful thing. It was the life essence and therefore precious. It communicated possession and power, and in the case of a feral wolf, it spoke of ownership and ancient magic. It bound the wolf to his mate and gave her power over him in return. It made them both stronger.

"I love you, Allie, and I always will," Rafe whispered in her ear as he settled beside her, finally able to remove himself from the warmth of her body. In his heart, he knew the warmth of her would linger long into this life and the next. He was sure of her now, as she had to be sure of him.

He saw Tim ease away from her too, getting up to run some water in the bathroom. He guessed his twin, much more together about Allie than he'd apparently been, was giving him a moment with her, and he silently blessed him.

Rafe rolled her so he could look down into her eyes.

"Did you hear me? I love you Allie, with all my heart."

She cupped his cheek and the expression in her soft eyes pulsed through her heart.

"I love you too, Rafe. I thought you knew that, but I don't mind your showing me at all. In fact, you can show me some more later, okay?" She lifted up wearily and kissed his mouth, then dropped her head back to the pillow. "But right now I'm going to be unconscious for a while." She smiled dreamily as she drifted off to sleep in his arms and he found himself grinning from ear to ear.

Tim found him that way, but Rafe didn't care. His twin knew him better than any being on the planet. They were a part of each other the way they were fast becoming part of Allie, only just slightly differently. They were two halves of the same soul. Allie was joining her soul to theirs, making them complete. It was an amazing gift.

Tim tossed a wet washcloth at him. It splatted against his chest while he was occupied watching Allie sleep. He looked up at his twin and grinned.

"She's an angel sent to earth. Isn't she, Tim?"

Tim stopped by his side of the big bed and his expression softened as he watched Allie sleep.

"You've got that right, Rafe." He pulled the blankets and comforter out from where they'd been kicked to the bottom of the bed and folded them neatly, ready to be pulled upward to cover them all. "Clean up our angel, then yourself. We need to catch some z's before we find a way to keep her—and all of us—safe."

The reminder of their predicament brought Rafe back to the moment. In the bliss that was Allie, he'd almost forgotten the cloud of threat hanging over them all. He took his brother's advice and softly petted their mate, cleaning her up so she wouldn't wake up sticky, then he padded out to the bathroom and did the same for himself.

When he got back to the bedroom, Tim had already released her hands from the cuffs and pulled the covers up over them, though Tim and he really didn't need the blankets at all. They were able to regulate their own body temperatures well enough that they were practically never cold. Still, Allie needed them and there was something very comforting about snuggling close under the covers with her in their arms.

Rafe padded up to his side of the bed and slipped under the blanket, glad when Tim raised no objection to his pulling Allie around to face him and snuggle deep into his arms. He needed this just now. Tim knew it and gave him space. There was no better man on earth, Rafe decided in that moment, than his twin, and no braver woman than their mate, Allie. She took them both on and never complained. Even when he turned all caveman on her, she took it mostly in stride and he loved her for it.

That thought firmly in mind, Rafe finally drifted off, getting the restful sleep he'd need to face the threat to his newly made family. No one would harm his mate. No one. He and his twin would see to it.

Chapter Twelve

Dante fed from the fey warrior who had been his friend centuries ago just as dawn kissed the sky. He then slipped into the death-like sleep of his kind. But for the first time, he had some—awareness, he guessed he would call it—of what transpired in the world around him while he was reduced to sleep. He actually felt the air heat as the sun brightened the sky, though the sun was still forbidden to him. Still, even this small thing would have moved him to tears had he been fully awake and able to express the emotions stirred in him by the first knowledge he had of the sun without pain in hundreds of years.

He had the half-fey blood powering his system to thank for it, he knew. He was also aware of other changes Duncan's blood was making in his ancient body. He felt the energies of the earth as never before, swirling around and through him, and he realized dimly in the haze of sleep, he could probably direct them with his will, if he so chose. The idea was startling.

Certainly Dante had already mastered some of the magic required to shapeshift, but never had he been so aware of the vast power of the earth and its creatures, or seen it so clearly. It was as if a veil had been lifted away from his eyes and only now was he seeing the reality of the world around him.

When he woke fully, just as the sun set, the differences were even more pronounced. While he'd slept throughout the day, Duncan's blood had integrated fully into his system, sharing its power and teaching him new ways of seeing, of sensing, of feeling. It was utterly amazing.

Duncan was there, watching him as Dante opened his eyes and began to breathe. The man stared down at him, his eyes assessing while Dante took in the golden glow surrounding the fey warrior. He was seeing his aura, he realized dimly in one corner of his mind, the immense energy that always surrounded the knight, in tangible form.

"Well?" Duncan asked, a concerned smile on his face. "Are you going to turn renegade on me and make me hunt you down?" He offered a hand to help Dante sit up. After due consideration, Dante took it.

"I think we can save that for later. Right now, I want to test these new powers you've given me." His head swam as he tried to rise too quickly from the cot in the run-down house he'd found and secured in a remote area just inside the national park. It was his safe house and he'd taken a chance bringing Duncan back here, but he thought he knew the knight well enough to risk it.

"Careful now." Duncan steadied him. "It might take a while to adjust. Can you tell me what you're feeling?"

"It's my eyes that are giving me trouble. I keep seeing this glow all around you. It's golden and bright. Like I imagine the sun might be if I were so blessed as to see it once more." He sat perfectly still, willing the dizziness to pass. "Your aura, right?"

"Hmm," Duncan agreed. "This is a good sign."

"Good for you maybe, but if the room would just stop spinning, I'd feel a whole lot better." The wry tone sparked Duncan's laughter and Dante was glad to have the knight there, though he'd been a loner for many centuries now. Since the loss of his brother, Dante hadn't wanted to let anyone near. Then Erik had befriended him almost against his will, and been ruthlessly slaughtered by the *were*. Since then, Dante had kept himself apart. He had no friends, but Duncan had been one—of sorts—centuries ago.

"I believe it will settle in time. You just have to get used to this new way of seeing. It's the way I see things, you know. Though I can usually turn it on and off at will. In time, you may learn the same control. This gift can be very helpful. Particularly in our current quest."

"Damn, I almost forgot how you knights always have to be on a quest of some sort or other. We don't do that in this day and age, my friend. You need to get with the times."

"Nonsense." Duncan clapped him on the back and went over to the small kitchen area, to pour himself a glass of water. He'd apparently gotten supplies for himself from somewhere, since Dante had little need of such amenities as food and water. "You also were once a knight, my friend. You can't have forgotten the thrill of the noble quest over these many years, any more than I."

"I've forgotten many things over the centuries, Duncan. I've deliberately tried to forget, but they keep coming back to haunt me."

Duncan sighed heavily from across the room. "You will not want to hear this, but I believe it is time you knew."

Dante's attention was snagged by the serious tone. "What is it?"

"There is no kind way to say this, so I will just say it plain. I think the *Venifucus* slew your brother and had something to do with the misunderstanding that ended in Erik's death."

"But why? What could they hope to gain?" Anger stirred in Dante's heart.

"It is my belief they've been trying long and hard to join you to their cause. One of your skill and strength would be a powerful weapon on their side. All they have done over these many centuries to hurt you and try to break your spirit could easily have resulted in your turning toward their side, if you'd been weaker of character."

"I'm no longer a knight, Duncan. I've done bad things in my time. My soul is far from pure."

Duncan had the gall to laugh. "Bad, perhaps, but evil? Purely evil? I think not, Dante. For then my blood would surely have poisoned you. I bespelled it so."

Dante sat back, stunned. "You took a big risk, Duncan. A poisoned vampire is a deadly one. If your blood had turned to poison in my body, I'd have been certain to kill you before I died."

Duncan nodded once, somberly. "It was a chance worth taking. Now I am even more certain of you and you've proven your purity of heart. We can move forward with no distrust between us."

"At least not on your side." Dante was more than a bit put out by the idea that his so-called old friend would test him in such a dangerous way, but on reflection he guessed he knew why the knight had done it. It had been centuries since they'd seen each other, after all. A lot could happen to change a man over such time. "What makes you believe the *Venifucus* have been targeting me through—" He trailed off, unable to complete the thought.

"Through your friends and family? Through the ones you loved?" Duncan sighed and moved forward to sit in a hard wooden chair he dragged over from the small dinette.

"When last we knew each other, it had been less than two centuries since your brother's untimely death. I took it upon myself to do a little investigating. As you should know—or will soon learn—the magical remnants can linger for centuries after certain events. The vile energies of murder linger longest of all. I found remnants of the Elspian Ring's murderous power all over your ancestral lands, Dante, and especially at the site of your brother's death. Remnants of his spirit lingered too. His death was no less than murder by magical means."

"And this Elspian Ring is what Vabian used to trick me into helping him, right? It's the same thing."

Duncan sighed. "A rare, evil, powerful thing, known only to a few. And now I have proof the *Venifucus* are using it. All the pieces start falling into place."

"What do you mean?"

Duncan stood abruptly. "No. I will say no more until we meet with the *were*lords. You all need to hear my fears at once to avoid...difficulties."

Dante scoffed. "Difficulties? What are you afraid of?"

"To be honest? That you'll go haring off on your own when together is the only way we even have a chance of stopping the wheels this Vabian has undoubtedly set in motion."

"If your theories are correct."

Duncan nodded, looking tired. "If my theories are correct, yes. But I fear with near certainty they are. Else the Lady would not have freed me at this time, in this place."

Dante mastered his spinning head and stood. "All right then, let's go back to those *were*wolves. The sooner I hear this mysterious theory of yours, the sooner we can all get to work killing that little weasel Vabian."

Duncan followed him out the door and to the truck without comment. Dante noticed immediately the presence of the *were*wolves watching his every move. Funny, he hadn't noticed them the night before, though he knew they must've followed him. Duncan and he were easy enough to follow in the big truck.

He'd known Tim and Rafe wouldn't let him wander around their territory without setting some sort of guard. What amazed him was the way his newly sharpened senses allowed him to pick out and identify each and every one of the *were* in the vicinity, even those in the trees above his head.

"If you'd rather ride than run, hop in the truck bed," Dante called with a chuckle, feeling the currents of surprise as he addressed the forest.

Only one brave soul padded forward to hop up into the truck bed and Dante knew he did it more as a statement than out of any sort of friendship. It was the priestess' uncle, Tom. How Dante knew that, when he'd never seen the man in his fur before, he didn't quite understand, but the knowledge was undeniable. He nodded to the cougar as he circled the truck bed until he found a comfortable spot and lay down.

"I'll try not to hit too many potholes, Tom." The cougar yowled once in acknowledgment and then settled down for the ride as Dante and Duncan loaded themselves into the wide cab.

"You sense them, don't you?" Duncan said softly when they were on their way.

Dante nodded. "It's amazing. I knew they were there before, but unless I actually saw them, I wouldn't have been able to tell where. Now I can feel them. Not just in general, but I know who they are. I can tell their energies one from the other. And I see the glow of energy all around them."

Duncan nodded. "They are powerful, blessed beings, for the most part. Every once in a while their powers get twisted somehow, or misguided, but most often, the *were* are honorable beings, blessed by the Lady. So it has been for more centuries than I have lived."

They pulled up to the small house set on the edge of the national park and Tom bounded out the back of the truck, heralding their arrival. The door opened and what looked like a much calmer Rafe greeted the two new arrivals.

"We've been waiting for you."

Dante felt a pang rush through him at the casual friendliness coming from the man. Friendship was something he hadn't allowed himself to experience in far too long. He'd been so hurt each time he'd let others into his life in any way, but it was time to try again. Dante knew this, but still it frightened him. There was very little in this world a vampire of his power could fear. Already though, this man and his brother were creeping into his awareness, as was their pretty mate. Without his volition, he knew if anything happened to any one of them, it would hurt him deeply.

Dante sighed, realizing it was far too late to worry about that now. They were already friends. All he could do at this point was help keep them as safe as possible so as to avoid the hurt he would feel if they fell victim to the evil he had unwittingly helped find them.

The war council was much as it had been the night before. The *were*folk had sent out scouts to search for Vabian, to no avail, it seemed.

"There is something else I must impart, and it bodes ill for us all." Duncan captured everyone's attention with his somber tone. "The presence of the Elspian Ring here and now ties in with things I learned when last I walked in this realm. The villain who murdered Elian d'Angleterre used this same forbidden magic. I found traces of it lingering at the site of the boy's death two centuries later. It had to be dark and violent magic indeed to leave such a trail."

"D'Angleterre?" One of the twins questioned softly. "Was he your brother?"

Dante nodded, unable to answer aloud and keep his façade of calm. Emotion rose in him, threatening to overwhelm his usual control.

"The lad was murdered by the same magic that is being used to hunt you now," Duncan said gravely, bringing everyone's attention back to him.

"So then the *Venifucus* killed Dante's brother centuries ago." Surprisingly it was one of the *were* twins who radiated understanding toward Dante.

Duncan nodded. "And it is my belief that the *Venifucus* also had a hand in the firewitch Erik's death that I've been told about."

"So they've been targeting Dante for centuries?" Rocky, the old grizzly sounded incredulous and humblingly sympathetic.

"I believe so." Duncan bowed his head slightly. "That means there is more afoot here than seems on the surface. The *Venifucus* target Dante, I believe, to try to turn him to their evil. He would be a strong ally for their cause." Suspicious eyes turned to regard Dante from all around the room, but Duncan went right on speaking. "They target the priestesses to eliminate any resistance, but they must be working toward some end, deeper than that which we see."

Grim faces showed all around.

"If the *Venifucus* are working toward some greater goal, we have to find out what it is if at all possible." Duncan's voice hardened with determination. "The safety of more than just this realm may be at stake."

Silence shrouded the room until one of the twins rose to gather the map and spread it out on the wide coffee table. The alphas all around renewed their efforts, focused now as never before.

Dante was seething inside, though he projected his usual calm demeanor. He'd perfected the air of tranquility over the centuries of his painful existence. Still, he understood Duncan's caution. If the *Venifucus* really were targeting him—and he felt certain at this point something like that was going on—then he owed them retribution for his brother's and Erik's deaths. Who knew what other tragedies in his long existence could also be laid at the feet of *Venifucus* agents? Vampire blood was slow to boil, but Dante was fast losing patience. He would hunt these *Venifucus* to the ends of the earth for what they'd done to those he loved. He would make them pay for their evil deeds and put a stop to them once and for all.

But he needed allies. Duncan, certainly, was his most powerful ally to date, but the *were*folk could not be discounted. Even though he'd felt no love for them in the past, Dante knew he could work with these twins to corner and kill Patrick Vabian. All of them had something at stake in this hunt, and he would work with them to bring Vabian to justice. After that though, the rest of the *Venifucus* were his—whether the *were*lords wanted to help or not.

"If we can get him here," Duncan was saying as he pointed to a spot on the topographical map. "I'll have a chance of banishing him to the Farthest Realm. This is a place of ancient power."

"You mean the circle of stones, right? That's the only thing that's up there and it's well hidden, overgrown in the forest.

Only the *were* know about it, or we'd be overrun with New Agers." Ryan rolled his eyes as he looked over the map with keen interest.

"Yes, a faerie ring on a large scale." Duncan nodded. "It could be of some use in trapping the mage. On our side, Dante is sure to be able to see the Elspian Ring now. He's growing accustomed to the new powers my blood has given him. He can watch from the sky and warn us of the mage's traps."

Dante chuckled from his standing position near the fireplace. "So that's why you did it."

"That's one of my reasons, old friend. There were many."

"Testing me among them," Dante challenged, still a little miffed at the cavalier way Duncan had toyed with his existence.

Duncan nodded gravely. "You should know," he turned to Rafe and Tim, "that my blood was bespelled. Had Dante been tainted by evil, it would have turned to poison in his system. His continued existence means he passed my test. His soul is still noble, though his sarcasm might have you believe otherwise."

"I already knew that." Tim surprised Dante by stepping forward. "I sensed it when he switched sides to help us protect Allie. And I knew it when I gave him my blood."

Duncan turned questioning eyes on him. "You have a blood bond with him?"

Dante nodded as the fey knight started to smile. "Then this will work out even better than I'd hoped."

CRSO

Allie woke after dark, deliciously sated and wonderfully sore in intimate places. She was warm and comfortable, and surprisingly clean, blushing as she realized her boys had taken care of her yet again.

After a quick shower, Allie dressed in comfy sweats and headed for the living room. She heard the masculine voices before she entered and something inside her shivered as she heard the relaxed note in Rafe's voice. It hadn't ever been there before. No matter how carefree he'd seemed, she realized hearing him now, he hadn't been fully at peace with their relationship...until now.

She felt a light in her heart as she thought of how precious he was to her, how dear. She was so happy she could give that to him, so glad to have his care and love in return. He'd made her feel cherished and needed in a way she'd never expected. His demands on her had been steep, but he hadn't gone too far, had been careful in fact, of pushing her beyond her boundaries, but together they'd all learned her boundaries went pretty far indeed. She blushed thinking about what they'd done to her, what she'd let them do and what she wanted them to do more of. She hadn't known she was so adventurous or kinky, but she was fast learning new facets of herself with these amazing men.

And they were hers. All hers.

Smiling, she entered the room and all eyes turned to her. Her uncles stopped her for a brief greeting, but no other dared waylay her on her way to her mates. She went to them, uncaring of those following her progress, and took her place between them on the wide couch.

"What did I miss?"

She kissed Rafe on the cheek, then turned to Tim, giving him the same light buss.

"We were just discussing the circle of stones," Duncan said with an elegant bow of his head in her direction.

"Oh, you mean that clearing where we went on Samhain for the ceremony?"

"The very same," came a soft, feminine voice from the entry by the hall. Duncan stood quickly and went over to the small woman, supporting her to a chair quickly vacated by one of the older *were* alphas.

"You should still be abed, cousin," Duncan chastised Betina softly as he settled her in the chair. She was wearing an oversized terry robe that had been left in the guestroom and a pair of Allie's fuzzy pink slippers.

"Resting in bed or resting here in this chair. It's all the same." She waved him away.

Allie stood and went to her side. "It is not, Betty, and you know it." Allie took the afghan from the back of the couch and tucked it around the older woman, careful of her injuries and mindful of how pale she still was.

"Oh, all right, but I'm needed here. My dear cousin is good, but he hasn't been in this realm in centuries and some things have changed that he might not recognize." Betty nodded significantly at her. "The role of women, being one." With a slight wink, Betty sent her back to the couch and captured the attention of everyone in the room. "Now what is this about the stone circle?"

Allie sat back down between her men, catching her breath when Rafe slid one of his hands onto her knee. Tim did the same on the other side and she waited to see if they would dare move their hands farther. Lucky for her sanity, they stayed right there on her knees, but their warmth was definitely distracting. And comforting.

"If we can get the mage to that place of power, we can trap him," Duncan was explaining.

"But how do you intend to get him there? He doesn't want any of you." Betina's shrewd eyes turned to Allie and the others in the room followed suit.

"He wants me," Allie said in a firm voice, sounding far braver than she felt inside. Yet, she knew she had to do this. She had to help in her own protection, to take an active role with the men she chose to spend her life with. She had to do this now, or she would forever be diminished, her status with the *were*folk somehow less. "I'll lead him into the trap."

"Like hell you will." Tim's growling voice carried through the room as his hand on her knee dug in almost painfully. Rafe's hand tightened too.

A show of force was required, she realized, and with the buildup of power she was experiencing, it would be easy enough. Directing it through her hands, she touched each of her mate's hands on her knees with a single, jolting finger. They immediately let go, clutching their tingling fingers to their chests as they scowled at her.

"What'd you do that for?"

Rafe sounded hurt more deeply than she would have guessed. She felt bad, but she knew she had to remain strong in the face of their anger. This was important. These next few weeks would set the tone for the rest of their years together and she had to start off on the right foot with both her mates and their people.

She stood, bringing Rafe's and then Tim's hands to her mouth and kissed them better. Using a little surge of her new power, she took the hurt away, soothing them with her healing touch.

"I'm sorry, but you need to know I'm not completely defenseless. I have power and a few skills now too. Maybe I don't have *were* senses, strength or speed, but I've got some abilities you don't and I'm not a weakling to be coddled and protected every moment of the day and night. I can't live like that. I won't."

"It's our duty to protect you." Rafe stood to face her, but Duncan came up beside them.

"And you'll do your duty whether she stays hidden here at home or follows her heart—and her Lady—to the stone circle. She is stronger than you know and just coming into her power. You diminish her if you do not let her grow."

"My cousin's right," Betina said softly, commanding all attention to her seated and bundled form. "Allie needs to do this. She needs to establish herself and her power, and she needs you to let her do it, boys. I know it goes against your nature, but you're alphas. You're stronger than your instincts. You can do this and by doing this, you will all grow and excel."

"If we don't all die first, that is." Tim's expression was guarded as he stood next to his twin, facing Allie. He ignored Duncan, focusing solely on his mate. "I don't like this plan at all."

Allie took both of their hands and brought them to her heart. "I know. And I know how hard it will be for you to see me in danger, but I know in my heart this is right. It's the only way we have to draw Vabian out into the open. If he follows me into the circle, you can spring the trap. You'll be with me every step of the way."

"You bet your ass we'll be with you," Rafe swore. "There's no way we'd let you go alone into the woods with no protection. We'll be at your side or we're not doing this at all."

She knew in that moment she'd won. They were willing to let her test her wings and she loved them all the more for it. Something inside her blossomed and swelled. It was love and it was something more—a power the likes of which she'd only felt once before, when she'd called on the Lady to heal Betina. It was vast, ancient and benevolent. And it was filling her with strength.

She reached up and kissed Rafe and then Tim on the cheek, smiling as bright as the sun. Her men would see her through. They could fight their natures to allow her this freedom, and she could let them dominate her in the bedroom. It was important to know their dominance was controllable, though she had no desire to change anything about their love life. No, she enjoyed letting them order her around in the bedroom too much to want to change a single thing about that. It was just in everyday life where she needed a little bit more freedom and she loved them even more for giving it to her.

"The three of us will lead him into the trap. Together," she promised them.

"And I'll be waiting in the stone circle to spring it," Duncan added from beside them.

Dante moved to their other side. "And I'll be watching from above to warn you of danger. You'll be guarded at all times."

The crackling energy of the Elspian Ring comforted Patrick Vabian as he watched the little house on the edge of the woods from a far-off vantage point. The *were* couldn't sense him though they prowled close at times, but his borrowed magic stood strong against them.

He'd seen that bastard vampire go into the house through his high-powered binoculars and cursed. The blasted bloodletter was working on their side now, but no matter. None of them could stand up to Patrick Vabian. He'd prove himself and bathe in their blood before taking his rightful place among the *Priori* of the *Venifucus*.

There was another with them now though, that he couldn't place. He'd been with Dante in the truck and walked into the house with him, welcomed by the *were*, but he wasn't *were*. Vabian wasn't quite sure what the newcomer was. Perhaps he was only human, though why supernaturals would be associating with a mere human escaped him. Still, he couldn't sense anything about the newcomer, so perhaps there really was nothing to sense. Or perhaps the man was hiding even more power than any of the others.

That thought gave him pause.

But his course was set. Vabian would heal up just a bit more, and then he would make his move. He had to get to the priestess. Only killing her would cement his place in the ranks of the *Priori*. He would kill her or die trying.

And Patrick Vabian didn't plan on dying anytime soon. Or at all, for that matter.

Chapter Thirteen

Everything was in place. Duncan and a contingent of *were*folk waited in and around the stone circle. Dante was already circling above in the form of a midnight black raven, his eyes sharp in the early evening dark, looking for any trace of the Elspian Ring as Duncan had taught him. Betina was well guarded back at the house and Tim and Rafe had silent escorts following their path as they walked with Allie, quickly and quietly through the forest to their destination.

This was the tricky part, Allie knew. Getting to the stone circle was the most vulnerable point of their plan. Once she was there, she'd be protected by the circle itself. It was a sacred place where few could harm her—a consecrated servant of the Lady. But the plan depended on getting her there in one piece, then luring Vabian after her into the circle where he could be trapped, questioned and punished. The power of the place was such that he would not be able to escape, even using such dark magic as the Elspian Ring.

They were almost there when Dante cried a warning from above. Tim and Rafe threw themselves at Allie as a surge of power knocked her off her feet and briefly into another dimension. When they emerged from the magical storm, they were miles away from the clearing where the circle of stones waited, clear on the other side of the mountain from their house, near a cave formation that was dark, dank and reeked of death.

Patrick Vabian greeted them with a sinister smile, but Allie refused to show her fear.

"It takes strong magic to transport us so far so fast. You have my compliments." Allie put on a brave smile, facing the man. She kept Tim and Rafe slightly behind her as she called on the vast resources now available to her. The shield she put between Vabian and herself extended to cover Rafe and Tim easily this time.

"I see you brought your two watchdogs with you. Pity, I really only wanted you."

Vabian sent off some magical bolts that would have hit her men if she hadn't been shielding. She felt the power slide off her newly strengthened shield and down into the earth to be reabsorbed. She also felt Vabian's consternation.

"Where she goes, we go," Tim said with some anger as he stepped to her side. Rafe did the same and she grabbed their wrists to keep them from leaving the safety of her shield.

Under her hands she felt them both shift half-way, preparing for battle. They had to keep Vabian occupied until their friends could find them. Dante could cover a lot of ground as a bird and Duncan could travel magically, just as Vabian had done. She just prayed they would find them quickly. Vabian was stronger than all of them, dangerous and powerful.

"Don't," she pleaded with her men. "Give them time." She couldn't say more with Vabian present.

"Our plan is shot to shit," Rafe said softly. "Now we just have to make the best of it. Remember I love you. I always will."

The half-wolf monster looked back at her with Rafe's eyes but she felt no fear. She knew it was her lover behind the fierce mask. She kissed his furry cheek, then turned to kiss Tim just before she let go of their hands. "I love you too."

Duncan cursed as he felt the surge of magical power a split second after he heard Dante's warning.

"Son of a bitch!" One of the *were*cougars nearby shouted, throwing off his clothing as he shifted to cat form and raced off through the forest, searching for them.

"Dante!" Duncan emerged from the stone circle to the spot where Rafe, Tim and Allie had just disappeared. The vampire floated down through the trees, now in human form, his silver eyes angry. "How strong is your connection with Tim? Can you sense him?"

Dante's eyes went blank as he searched inside, then triumph flared. "They're not far."

"*Were*folk!" Duncan sounded the battlecry as the *were*creatures in the woods rallied to his call. "Follow us!"

Dante shifted to wolf form as he bounded through the forest, the fey knight moving faster than any human could, right behind him. Around them was a small army of *were* in various forms, all angry and ready for battle. Patrick Vabian wouldn't know what hit him. If they could just get there in time.

Dante arrived at the cave mouth first, taking in the raging battle with one quick glance before launching himself into the fray. Allie stood back, shielding herself and her men as best she could while Rafe and Tim stalked the mage. He threw fire and directed killing blows with the silver knife that even yet dripped with blood while Allie did all she could to counter the blows before they struck home.

She was good, but not fast enough. Every once in a while a particularly vicious blow would get through her guard to hurt her or one of her mates. They were fading fast, the *were*wolves bleeding from nasty gashes even as Vabian clutched his own battered and bloodied arms close to his sides.

Dante saw his opening and went for it. Sweeping in from the side, he bit clean through the mage's wrist, taking the hand and the blade it held with him as he landed hard on the forest floor beyond. The mage's blood tasted sweet in his mouth, but the stink of evil from the silver blade made him drop the bloody trophy in the dirt. A moment later, he shifted back to his human form.

Vabian howled in pain and tried to run now that his most powerful weapon was gone, but the *were*wolves had him pinned.

"Patrick Vabian." Duncan stepped into the clearing, his voice strong, his appearance followed by dozens of *were* in all shapes and sizes. The mage's eyes widened in horror. "For the crimes you've committed against priestesses of the Lady, you are condemned. Do you have anything to say for yourself?"

Vabian began to chant, but it was a dark, evil thing, and Duncan cut him off with a gesture. The half-fey warrior sealed the mage's lips with powerful magic, even as Tim choked off the man's air supply. Tim's huge, half-wolven hand nearly crushed Vabian's throat.

Duncan stepped right up to the man and motioned Tim away. The *were*wolf complied grudgingly.

"I will make your end easy if you will but tell me who taught you of the Elspian Ring."

Vabian laughed almost hysterically. "She will destroy you all!"

Rafe started forward, pressing his claws into the man. "She?"

"Elspeth. The *Mater Priori*. She's coming for you and she'll send you all to your deaths!"

Duncan went pale, but Dante caught his friend from behind, shoring him up. Whatever this fool was blabbing about, it had to be some serious shit to make the fey warrior react so strongly.

"*Courage, mon ami,*" he whispered to the knight in the language they had once shared, centuries before.

Seeing the glint of the silver blade on the ground, Duncan went over to it. The blood of *were*, vampire and priestess alike stained its surface and it fairly glowed with the evil intent of its wielder. It must be destroyed.

Summoning his power, Duncan sent a flash of magical energy into the blade, shielding it at the last minute lest any of his companions be hit with even a trace of the deadly silver. He sent the energy of the blade back into the earth to be dispersed as he did the silver itself, disintegrating it with his power and embedding each molecule into the rock deep down under the earth where it could harm none ever again.

Were and vampire alike breathed a sigh of relief when the poisonous weapon was gone. Duncan noted their reactions as he turned back to the mage. The two alpha *were*wolves were at his throat once more.

"You threatened our mate," Rafe said in a growly, half-human voice. "For that alone, you die."

"Let the Lady cleanse him." The soft, feminine voice came from behind the gathered men, silencing them. "Bring him to the stone circle."

"It's too far away," Rafe said softly, turning to her, but she only smiled.

"Duncan can take him there in the blink of an eye." She held out her hands to her two mates. "And I can take you."

"You can?" Tim asked uncertainly.

Allie nodded at him. "I can now that I've felt how it's done. Trust me, my loves. This is what's meant to be." She grasped their hands in hers and in a vast blink of her power, they were gone, along with many of the *were*folk.

Duncan realized she'd taken as many as she could, lightening his load considerably. Still, as a knight of faerie, he had power to spare. Taking a tight hold on the villain, Duncan used his power to transport him directly to the center of the stone circle.

The ancient, living stones groaned at the presence of such evil, but Duncan sent out a wave of his calming power to quiet them. He was relieved to see Allie and her mates as well as the *were*folk there before him. She'd already begun consecrating the circle, just waiting for their arrival to seal it. He felt it close with a lash of her power, impressive now that she was finally coming into her own.

He let go of Vabian, sure the man could not escape. He was sealed within the circle, just as surely as they were, but just to be sure, he stayed nearby. He noticed Dante took up position on one side of the mage, while he guarded the other. The alpha twins guarded their mate who faced the mage across the stone altar. Assorted *were* eyes watched from all around the circle, witnessing and guarding.

"Patrick Vabian, you stand for your crimes before the Lady now. She will be your judge, jury and executioner, if She so wills." Allie's voice carried across the clearing, ringing through the stones that welcomed her fresh, new power with joy.

"Do you repent of your evil ways?" Duncan prodded the man.

"I serve the *Mater Priori*. She will defeat your Lady."

"You are so wrong." Allie shook her head. "So misguided. You could have had Her compassion and love. Instead you chose evil."

She stepped up to the middle of the stone altar and Rafe and Tim stood at either end beside her. Allie raised her hands and rainbows of light filtered down through the night air as her beautiful voice lifted in a pure, clear chant, ringing across the stones. The power intensified as Vabian staggered to his knees in the center of the ring, covering his ears.

Still, Duncan stood guard, as did Dante, seemingly unafraid of the swirling magic. Duncan was proud of the little woman who had grown so fast into her amazing power. He didn't know if she was finished evolving yet, but even so, her strength was amazing. She called on the earth, the forest and sky, but most of all she called on the goodness of the Lady she served. He watched in awe as the enormous power she commanded swirled out and down, arcing off every one of the standing stones and into the mage cowering before them.

Vabian was cleansed. That's the only word Duncan had for it. He actually felt the evil power of him being drained away into the earth until nothing was left behind but an empty shell of a man. Then that man too, disappeared in a poof of light and power, sent to another realm for atonement, or perhaps a second chance, Duncan didn't know which. Such choices were up to the Lady alone.

When the light cleared, Patrick Vabian was gone from their midst, the circle cleansed of his evil taint and pure power flowed once more unhindered through the earth beneath them. Allie faced them with an odd mix of sorrow and triumph on her pretty face.

"You've done well, milady," Duncan told her, knowing she needed reassurance, but he needn't have bothered.

Her mates were instantly at her side, crowding close, hugging her to them as she swayed on her feet. So much power flowing through one so new to it must have been disorienting, but she was in good hands now.

"Is he dead?" Rafe asked, searching for evidence of the mage's fate even as he comforted his mate.

"I think not," Dante said, moving forward to where the man had disappeared.

"He's been cleansed of all magic," Duncan nodded even as he concentrated on the power buildup in the area, "and sent, I suspect, to the Farthest Realm or one near to it."

"Not a fun place, I take it?" Tim asked as he wrapped one thick arm around Allie's waist.

"Even if he could return from such a place, his power has been drained. He is of no use to the *Venifucus* or threat to us. That's the most important point, I think."

Duncan finished the task of releasing the energies back to the earth, then dispersing the magical circle. Within moments, they were all heading down the mountain toward the small house on the edge of the woods.

Betina was waiting for them, ensconced comfortably on the couch as they walked in. Her eyes were alight with eagerness for news, though she certainly had felt the power discharge as the mage was dispersed.

"How did it go? Any losses on our side?" Concern laced her tone.

Tim and Rafe ushered Allie to the small loveseat opposite the couch, seating themselves first, then pulling her across their laps. Broad grins covered both their handsome faces.

"You should've seen her, Betina. Our girl is amazing." Rafe kissed her cheek, licking her neck as she giggled.

"I'm glad you think so," Allie said on a laugh, then faced her mentor. "To answer your question, nobody was seriously hurt on our side, though Tim has some scratches." Allie bent to examine Tim's ripped shirt, but he intercepted her, pulling her in for a lingering kiss and sidetracking her attention. Betina was glad to see them so frisky. She sighed as she looked to the door, noting each new arrival.

Duncan came and knelt at her side, his expression grim. Dante stood at the fireplace, his habitual spot now that he was welcomed inside this home. The other *were* filtered in, nodding respectfully to her, each with varying expressions of wonder, consternation, worry and hope on their faces. It was a confusing mix.

"What's wrong?" Betina asked Duncan very quietly.

"The mage spoke before he was dispersed," Duncan said softly, all eyes turning to him. "He spoke of an ancient evil."

"Who's the woman he mentioned?" Tim wanted to know.

"Elspeth was once known as the Destroyer of Worlds," Duncan said softly, his gaze holding Betina's as she gasped. "She was banished to the Farthest Realm for her wickedness, but her servants remained hidden. Only now do I see the link between her and the *Venifucus*. It should have been obvious to me before."

"Are you certain? It was Elspeth he spoke of?" Betina wanted to be very sure before allowing the terror to rise in her mind.

"I'm certain. He named her and called her the *Mater Priori.* All this time, she's been the one behind the *Venifucus.* That's where her left-behind servants gathered, biding their time and plotting. I can't believe I didn't see it!"

Betina sighed, trying to remain calm. "Don't blame yourself, Duncan. No one knew or even suspected the connection. You've done a good thing here, eliciting the information from Vabian." Betina's tone was soft. "A new era is upon us. A very dangerous time for us all."

About the Author

To learn more about Bianca D'Arc, please visit http://biancadarc.com. Send an email to Bianca D'Arc at Bianca@biancadarc.com or join her Yahoo! group to join in the fun with other readers as well as Bianca D'Arc! http://groups.yahoo.com/group/BiancaDArc/.

Look for these titles

Now Available:

Dragon Knights Book 1: Maiden Flight
Dragon Knights Book 2: Border Lair
Dragon Knights 1 & 2: Ladies of the Lair (print collection)
Dragon Knights Book 3: The Ice Dragon

Coming Soon:

Forever Valentine
Dragon Knights 4: The Prince of Spies
Hara's Legacy

Ancient, eternal, magikal, and in love with a woman immune to his charms. The combination can bring even the strongest druid sorcerer to his knees.

Sacred Places
© *2006 Mandy M. Roth*

Ancient, eternal, magikal, and in love with a woman immune to his charms. The combination can bring even the strongest druid sorcerer to his knees.

Coyle O'Caha, a seven-hundred-year-old, immortal druid sorcerer, has one claim to fame—his experience mentoring fledgling witches. Three years ago, he found his soulmate, Deri Sullivan. With Deri haunting his dreams, he can no longer wait to claim her. He's tired of waiting for her to fall for his charms and see that he's the man for her. Of course, that's easier said than done since Deri is immune to both his charm and magik.

Deri Sullivan's boss is a real piece of work. Not only is Coyle a millionaire with a body to die for and an attitude to match, but he also has a Scottish lilt which makes her knees weak. He's a certified ladies' man. A man she should avoid at all costs. A man she can't seem to quit dreaming about. A man with whom she wishes she could share her secret. Sometimes love happens at its own pace, other times, a supernatural nudge is needed.

WARNING: This book contains hot, explicit sex and violence explained with contemporary, graphic language.

Available now in ebook and print from Samhain Publishing.

Enjoy the following excerpt from "Sacred Places"...

Only Coyle made her body react this way and it seemed to be getting worse as time went on. What had started off as mere curiosity on her part now bordered on obsession. He consumed her waking thoughts and seemed to invade her every dream. It had to end soon. She had someone else in her life. Someone who wasn't unobtainable. Someone who claimed to care for her even though he had a funny way of showing it. Why was she drawn to this moody millionaire who still insisted on running his own small pub on the seaside?

Sure, his devilishly handsome good looks had something to do with it. How could they not? The man's black tousled hair hung just past his ears and it looked as untamable as the rest of him. The seemingly endless tribal tattoos adorning his body added a whole new layer to Coyle's mystique. Setting aside his money, he was pure perfection. He also had the ability to not only make her feel safe, which was rare, but to make her laugh as well.

You and every other babe out there.

Women flocked to him. It was sickening. They arrived at the pub in groups of four or more, retreating to the back with Coyle until the wee hours of the morning. Deri refused to be one of his endless streams of women. She was not a Coyle groupie nor would she ever be one.

Okay, maybe not outwardly, but inwardly I'm a classic groupie.

Disgusted by her lack of willpower, Deri steeled herself to his touch, hoping it would make her immune to whatever it was he possessed. It didn't. It did, however, make her painfully aware of how close she was to being one of his groupies.

I will not throw myself at this man's feet.

Jerking back from him, Deri shook her head, sending tendrils of red hair scattering about as her clip gave way. Her hair seemed to engulf Coyle's large hands as it fell to the tips of her breasts, teasing her and driving her closer to the brink of begging him to have her.

The sound of her cell phone ringing caught her attention and saved Deri from making an even bigger fool of herself. Drawing back more, she tipped her head. "Excuse me."

"Of course," Coyle bit out, aggravation evident. "Wouldnae want to keep precocious lil' Chad waiting."

Rolling her eyes, she pulled her cell phone from her waist. "As if you have any clue who is calling me." She flipped her phone open. "Hello?"

"Hey, Deri," Chad said, his voice strained. For a split second, Deri thought she heard a female's voice in the background, whispering something low near Chad. She dismissed the thought although her mind tripped over it once more.

"Umm, hi." She turned and tried to walk away from Coyle to avoid his penetrating stare. Plus, putting distance between herself and the headstrong Scot would only help to avoid letting him know he was right about who was on the phone. Though, Deri had little doubt the man needed no such confirmation.

Wonderful. Sexy and psychic.

Coyle moved with her, dwarfing her five-foot, six-inch frame with his close to six and a half feet one. The slightest bit of pressure from his hands was enough to hold her in one spot, not that she wanted to go too far from him anyway. No. Deri wanted to be pinned beneath those hands. Held in place as he used his long fingers to explore every inch of her.

Take me.

A cocky smile graced Coyle's face. The urge to smack it off was great. She held back. "Tell Chad I said 'hi.'"

Before she could stop herself, Deri had her middle finger in the air—flipping Coyle off in a very unladylike gesture. Coyle nipped playfully at it. "Promises. Promises, Deri. If it's rutting yer after you've only but to ask. I'll nae deny you." He ran a hand over the bulge in his jeans and arched a brow. "I wouldnae suggest being fool enough to tempt me again or you might find yerself spread out before me like an offering. And, lass," he added in a low voice, "I'll do more than take you up on it. I'll consume you."

Her jaw dropped. Coyle captured her middle finger with his mouth and sucked gently, sending sparks of pleasure through her body. Instantly, her inner thighs tightened. She gasped. He chuckled as he worked his tongue out and over her finger with a skill she could easily imagine him utilizing to bring her pleasure.

"Deri?" Chad asked. "Babycakes, you okay?"

"What woman are you with now?" The question made little sense but it fell from her lips all the same. Still, it was all she had and the feeling that Chad wasn't alone nagged her. It had been over a year since someone, besides herself, had touched her in a way that was even remotely sexual. To have the one man she desired most doing it was almost too much.

"What woman?" Chad laughed. It sounded forced, with a nervous edge. "Deri, I called to tell you that I'm running late and stuck at the office. There is no other woman. I won't be able to pick you up from work tonight. Can you catch a ride home with Gigi?"

Coming to her senses, she yanked her finger from Coyle's mouth and shook her head. "No, I can't get a ride home with Gigi because she's off tonight and tomorrow and the next night," she mentally counted to five before continuing on, "because she's visiting her sister in Pennsylvania, Chad. Remember? You were with me when I dropped her off at the bus depot."

It would have been so easy to zap Chad with her power. Too easy. Killing mortals was wrong. She didn't need anyone to tell her as much. *Inflicting a little pain on the other hand—no, I can't.*

Discover eBooks!

THE FASTEST WAY TO GET THE HOTTEST NAMES

Get your favorite authors on your favorite reader, long before they're
out in print! Ebooks from Samhain go wherever you go, and work with
whatever you carry—Palm, PDF, Mobi, and more.

WWW.SAMHAINPUBLISHING.COM